And Still She Stayed

And Still She Stayed

By

Chloe Ramsay

ISBN: 978-1-0676267-0-9

Also available as an eBook

Website and cover design: Chloe Ramsay - Dave Palmer Consulting:
www.davepalmerconsulting.co.uk
Stylistic line editing: Rachael Palmer
Proofreading, Formatting and Printing: DPC Printing Group Limited

For the girls who were told silence was safety

They taught her that obedience was safety and that quiet girls were spared the worst of the world. They did not tell her that silence has a cost, or that some houses survive by consuming the women inside them. History remembers the men who owned the land and name. It forgets the girls who learned how to leave.

Chapter One

The Letter

January 1816

Eliza's bedroom was freezing; the chill seeped through the thin panes of glass that rattled faintly in the winter gusts… yet she hardly noticed. Her eyes were wide with curiosity burning through the pages like a laser. She followed the curly letters in the worn book, cradling it in her arms like it was her precious baby. Outside in the pale winter town, it was silent. Eliza had her face buried in the books long before the world had even started their day. She loved to read so much because there were so many amazing stories (non-fiction and fictional) to get away and escape into a new world, they stay with you everywhere no matter if you were awake or asleep. The new world could be anything from flying unicorns to pirates fighting, the possibilities are endless and you get to decide what world you go into.

The fire behind the grate was little bit more than a glow, a few stubborn pieces of wood grasping for life creating a kind of roaring and crackling that was silenced behind the bars like a prisoner. A swift draft of frigid air tiptoed along the cracked oak floorboards, tugging at threadbare curtains, the frayed edges dancing like ballerinas and a few bits quietly frayed even more. Meanwhile the soft scented candle's flame stood defiantly against the draft and the dark. Eliza turned the page vigorously, her mind slipping out of reality and into the world of words where you can see them floating off the pages into your mind's eye creating wonderful views of faraway lands. A perfect refuge from the weight that she carried on her shoulders and in her young naïve heart.

She had read this particular book way too many times to count, in fact she had read all of the stories about distant countries, horrible kings and a girl who always outwitted them all. The spine had cracked long ago, and the corners were stained from slightly oily fingers too eager to be careful with the next page. She ran her finger lightly over one sentence she liked to reread all the time:

"There is no magic in fate, only in those who dare to rise from it."

Her lips moved silently over the words, creating it into her own sort of affirmation. Eventually, the house began to make noise from downstairs; the low whispers of voices, clatter of dishes and the slow creaking of floorboards as if they were trying not to wake Eliza.

She had noticed that the aroma in the house slowly changed from burnt wood and dust to weak tea and homemade bread, coaxing Eliza from her reading trance. She closed the book gently, careful not to crease the fragile pages even more so than they already were. Then blew out the candle with as much might as her frozen lungs tried their hardest to follow through. In the silence that followed, she stood up and smoothed out her creased sea-green linen skirt she was wearing and made her way out of her room, down the stairs, past the living room and into the kitchen.

The kitchen was a modest sized room, that at first glance appeared bare and uninviting, but efforts had been made to make it semi-homely. In the middle was a rough beaten-up oak table scarred by years of use, with a couple of wax candles sitting on a frayed yellowish cloth runner carefully placed down the middle of the oak table. A comforting fire that was heating the room was to the left of the table, its warmth seeping into the cold bones of not just the family but the house itself. Around the table, the household had gathered: Eliza, Eliza's mother Maggie, her younger brother, Samuel, and a few friends from the town. Sadly, Samuel's father and Maggie's husband, Kenneth had passed away from pneumonia the year before. They all missed him particularly Samuel, who had taken to inviting random friends for breakfast.

"Morning, love," Maggie murmured, half awake, dusting flour off her hands reaching for the loaf she had just pulled from the oven. Her black apron was covered in white handprints and her face red from the heat of the oven. Eliza returned the greeting with a tired smile then took her seat at the end of the bench.

Breakfast was quiet, the dull sounds of spoons against wooden bowls, soft tearing of bread and the slow chewing that comes along with breakfast was all that was heard. Eliza ate slowly (almost as if she were in slow motion), her thoughts drifting back into the land of books. Her younger brother Samuel jabbered on about catching a hare that had snuck past the fence, but Eliza only listened absently, her eyes were drawn to the window where the trees danced, and chilly wind harmonised with the birds. It was a morning like many others yet there was a heaviness in her chest, and her heart told her that something was coming. Not a might but a was.

Then, as the sun rose higher and the house settled into their routines, a background sound disturbed the calm. The sharp tap of paper fluttering against the door. There was only the family in the kitchen. Maggie frowned and wiping her hands on her apron, she crossed the room quickly and she unlatched the door. The chilly morning air swept in with a sudden whoosh while a single envelope, thick and creamy, fluttered feather-like onto the floor waiting to be picked up and read.

"It's for you, Eliza." Maggie gasped.

No one other than Maggie ever got letters.

Eliza rushed over in a hurry of excitement, her heart already pounding with a strange thrill. She bent to retrieve the letter from the floor near her mother's feet. Her fingers trembling as she saw the wax seal pressed deeply and carefully: a crown surrounded by twisted vines.

'The crest of the Harrow family…' She whispered in disbelief, surprised that they would even know who she was, let alone send a letter directly to her.

Seeing the crest alone was enough to steal the breath away from her organs. She turned it over in her hands feeling the weight of it, it was much heavier than ordinary post. This left her puzzled of what it could be about.

'Well, open it then!' Samuel yelled impatiently. 'Open it!' His voice had become louder and sterner.

Eliza broke the seal with care, unfolding the letter inside. The script was precise and rich, inked with certainty and elegance. Eliza read out the letter, her tone low and shaky:

Miss Eliza Fell,
You are hereby summoned to Greywick House to tutor the Master's daughter, Clara Harrow.
Your presence is required without delay.
Miss Janet Mary Williams (Greywick Estate Maid)

A long silence followed, Maggie's face had turned ghostly white. 'No,' she said softly. Her hands clutched tightly at the doorframe as if to hold herself up from falling. 'No… no, not there!'

Eliza looked up, confusion knitting her brows tightly. 'Why? What is it mother?'

'You must not go!' Maggie whispered urgently, her voice trembling more and more. 'Not to the Harrow estate. Not now. Not ever!'

'But it's an honour!' Eliza replied still holding the letter tightly. 'It must be… it says I am to tutor their daughter I will be paid surely. It means they have heard of me, of how I did at the parish school.' Eliza said excitedly.

Maggie shook her head; her eyes were glassy and staring not at but through Eliza. 'You do not know what they are, the Harrows. They are not like other people that place eats folk like us!'

The kitchen fell silent again but there was an uneasy atmosphere, though Eliza still felt excitement rushing through her body. An anxious, excited thrill. Greywick. The Harrows. A huge estate at the edge of the hills, full of stories, mystery, danger even. It did not frighten her the way it should have, if anything, it lit something inside her. Something bold and daring.

'Isn't this what you've always said though?" She asked gently but firm. "That I was not made to spend my life boiling linen and feeding chickens?"

Maggie's jaw clenched hard, grating her teeth together. "Not like that. Not *there*."

But Eliza was already smoothing its lines perfectly, folding the letter back up and tucking it into her pocket like a secret. "If it means I get to learn, teach, have something that's mine…"

She did not finish the sentence. She did not need to.

Later that day, the house was still filled with tension. Maggie hardly spoke and when she did it was short stern warnings: pack warm clothes, do not wander, do not go near the old wing. She would not explain why apart from saying that Eliza would know soon enough.

That night Eliza could not sleep. She lay curled up beneath her white thin woollen blanket, staring at the ceiling beams, the letter on the table beside her. Her mind spun around with all of the possibilities: 'What kind of girl was Clara Harrow?' 'What did they want from her?' 'Why do they need her a tutor?' 'What secrets are at Greywick?' and so forth. She had only heard of Greywick and the Harrows in snippets like things whispered at market stalls, or hushed conversations that were quicky stifled whilst passing through the streets... Apparently, Lord Harrow was an only child and had inherited the estate and title when he was just fourteen years of age after a terrible accident had occurred while the family were travelling, he was the only survivor… but that was all. The wind picked up outside making the damp shutters creak and the candle flicker again. A white mouse scuttles into a small hole in Eliza's wall too. But it was not the sounds that kept Eliza awake. She would go; she had to. There was no staying still, not now.

She reached under her flat feathered pillow and pulled out a faded silver pendant with no photo inside. It was a gift from her mother. Her fingers brushing off the slight dust that had gathered on it from being under her pillow and cupped it in her hands like she was making a wish. She then traced the lines that swirled around to form a design. She murmured,

"You are hereby summoned… your presence is required."

She realised it did not ask, it told. No kindness, apology nor beg. Just a statement of must. Her name was written in ink carefully, as if the person who wrote it knew who she was. Not just her name. *Her.* A hundred questions crowded her brain once again but this time with slightly different questions: 'Why her?' 'Why now?' 'Who told them she could teach or that she could be trusted?' She was just an ordinary girl with no connections to the aristocracy.

She laid back again staring at the ceiling counting the cracks in the beams. A breath was let out creating a small fog in the air. She thought of Maggie's face drained of colour.

"You must not go... not to the Greywick estate. Not now."

Not *now*. Why not now? And why did she dislike them so much? Eliza had so many questions filling her head constantly but no answers.

As the early morning light spilled through the window illuminating the letter on the table still beside her, Eliza knew that nothing would ever be the same again.

She would read before anyone had woken up, braid her hair, polish her boots, and then pack a worn satchel with two books and her silver locket.

She would kiss her mother and brother on the forehead and step outside the cottage door. But for now, in the dawn, Eliza just crawled through her thoughts and started reading. Far off beyond the town and hills, Greywick waited as if it was one of her many unread books.

Chapter Two

On The Road

Eliza rose before the frost had a chance to clear from the windowpanes, she always does. The house was still dim and silent. She sat beside the window with numb fingers, braiding her hair into a messy plait due to her fingers trembling. Beneath her breath she muttered verses from memory, lines from an old ballad; lyrics she had half-learned from overheard songs and the pages of books she read. The rhythm soothed her more than sleep ever had done.

Her boots were quietly polished to perfection during the night, with the last bit of lamp oil and a beige dirt-spotted ragged cloth sat near the already-made bed. She laced them slowly, pulling the knots tight and secure. Her satchel was wide open on the chair and half packed. It had two books (one of Latin verbs, one fiction), a folded outfit and a woollen scarf her mother warned her to bring.

She tucked her silver locket between the pages of one of the books like she was hiding it. The pendant had belonged to her grandmother, passed down, and now worn around Eliza's neck since she was much younger. Though it felt heavier today. She added her faded ribbon (the one Maggie had said made her look “almost proper”) and her bonnet, stiff from dust but was brushed clean and laid on top of the satchel.

Downstairs, the house still was sleeping. The smell of barley porridge and damp stone filled the room faintly. Eliza stirred the pot absently; her thoughts were elsewhere. When Samuel entered, yawning and rubbing his eyes, she jumped out of her skin. Then she giggled and set a bowl in front of him on the old oak table.

Soon enough the goodbye came, though it did not feel right nor sincere. Without making a fuss Maggie stood by the door, her hands folded and wrapped in her apron, her eyes narrowed… lowered to the floor. Eliza kissed her cheek gently, in a ‘I am doing this, but I still love you’ kind of way.

‘Write to us,’ Samuel spoke low, voice cracking with something that was not just a lack of sleep. It was more emotional than that.

‘I will.’ Eliza gulped holding back her tears welling up in her eyes.

Eliza stepped outside into the crisp morning air, her breath floating in clouds above and next to her. The sky was a dull, flat grey. Quite boring really. The road shimmered a little with frost and at the end of the lane a carriage waited for her. The new journey of her life.

It stood still and silent like a thing carved from coal. Its black outer paint gleamed despite the mist and its high dome roof made it look like a royal hearse than a tutor’s transport. The horses snorted into the cold, stamping their hooves in coordination as the coachman dismounted effortlessly. He gave her no greeting beyond a simple nod. His coat was way too large and his hat was pulled exceptionally low leaving only a nose and beard visible to Eliza.

Slowly she stepped out and down the lane before she turned and glanced back at the house, Maggie had not followed her out and only Samuel stood on the doorstep, his arms crossed shivering in the cold. She waved and he raised his hand. Maggie did not appear anywhere, not even peering from a window to say goodbye to her daughter. The coachman opened the door and Eliza climbed up, skirt gathered together so it did not catch on anything. She would have to sit on a cold leather seat for the whole journey. The door shut harshly.

The carriage began to move, slowly at first but eventually the wheels gained momentum crunching over the dry earth and frozen puddles along the way. The fog hugged the trees tightly, suffocatingly. Inside Eliza sat stiffly, her ice-cold hands folded in her lap with her satchel resting next to her. She patted it lightly now and then to remind herself it was there, maybe to ease anxiety.

Eliza tried to read but after she had opened one of her books and read the first line three times, she knew she could not retain it or focus. It was not the cold that bit her. It was the silence, the unknown. She leaned against the carriage window watching the countryside hills pass by in shades of grey, brown, and white. Cottages stand beautifully with winter dressed on top of their roofs like a fresh sheet of linen. They passed an area where tree stumps dotted the land and men were working with their axes to fell the remaining trees. The coachman driving the carriage said very little. He did mutter something about turning off the main road soon enough once, but Eliza only replied with a nod which he could not see.

The road narrowed and twisted, the trees grew taller and darker, the fog thickened. Everything about this new path and direction was eerie yet she chose to go. Occasionally they would pass a crossroad or a leaning rotten signpost with worn and flaked paint. Eliza tried to read them, but they passed too quickly for her to see properly.

Suddenly and unrelatedly, a memory surfaced into Eliza's mind. It was her mother years ago standing by the fire.

'Eliza?' Maggie had said, 'not all roads lead back, remember?'

She did not understand what she had meant then, but now alone in a carriage with a stranger waiting to arrive at a place even her mother feared, she thought she might be starting to understand.

As they climbed higher into the hills, the view started to change slightly. It was no longer farmland, but stone walls mossy and crumbling. When she looked out of the window, she saw a ruined chapel with the roof caved in, windows hollowed out and a crow sat carefully on the edge of a broken cross.

By midday the clouds had thickened like the fog, the air was strangling and damp. Her fingers hurt from coldness despite her winter gloves. She had stopped trying to read and stared aimlessly out the window instead, entering books through her mind as that was easier than actually reading.

The horses started to slow little by little, the carriage creaked and groaned as the road became rougher and felt less travelled.

They passed underneath a hanging branch that scraped the top of the roof like fingernails on chalkboard.

Then she saw it.

Not Greywick, not yet, but the first sign of its existence. A wooden rotted marker, barely standing that had half sunk into the mud where two narrow roads forked in separate ways. The carving was a little faded, but she could just about make out the word:

GREYWICK

Her positioning and manner changed in an instant after seeing the sign. She sat upright as if her back was stuck to the chair while clenching her jaw shut, her stomach began twisting like she might bring up her breakfast. She had never experienced motion sickness before.

The trees around her leaned in closer and the road turned a sharp left into the thick fog. Eliza started to question her decision after all, but it was too late to turn back now because the Harrows would know that she was spooked and had left. The carriage continued on and on. Whatever lay ahead was no longer a place heard on the streets or in the books. It was real and it was waiting for her arrival.

Soon she will be another chapter in the story.

Chapter Three

Estate that Sees

The sign tipped a bit as they passed because of the gust of winds, it read:

"GREYWICK"

Another sign came into view, being buffeted by the wind. This sign was much clearer than the last as it was made of wrought iron, more sturdy, though it was twisted with the silver of the iron and slivers of orange dripped down the wooden post it was attached; however, this sign was much clearer than the wooden one not too long ago so she thought they must be getting nearer.

Eliza pressed her face to the glass. Mist and fog curled across the road ahead like fingers forcefully pulling them in. Trees lined the path now, taller, and denser, their trunks coated with thick slimy moss, which shimmered ethereally due to the constant damp. The air seemed thicker here too as if it knew not to breathe too loudly or deeply. The carriage bumped along the grey cobbled road, wheels groaning with each rotation like it was too tired to continue. Even the horses had become quieter, their pace slowing without being told to by the coachman leading.

Then she saw it, she marvelled and her jaw dropped literally not figuratively.

She saw the estate.

Greywick did not sit on the land, it ruled it. Huge and dark, with more windows than she could count and towers that disappeared way up into the foggy clouds and sky. Ivy and moss covered most of it as if it were abandoned, creeping across the stone like it wanted to hold the house… to keep it contained. The front doors were tall heavy-looking, arched like it was the entrance to something old and important. Something waiting. It was ugly in a beautiful way. Sharp and watchful like it had eyes.

The carriage stopped with a sudden jerk; Eliza's satchel knocked against her side as she fell forward bracing her hands out. She stepped out slowly. Her newly perfectly polished boots sank a little into the damp mottled gravel coating it in a dusty mud. All of a sudden there was a sharpness straight to the lungs, but it was not the cold that hit her. It was the silence. There were no birds. No wind. Just the sound of her own body moving and breathing as well as the faint creak of the carriage.

The front door opened before she had a chance to go up and knock. A woman stood there. Grey apron, sleeves rolled, hair pinned back so tight it looked painful. Her face did not change when she saw Eliza… no smile, no welcome.

'Eliza Fell?'

'Yes,' Eliza replied politely but quietly.

'My name is Janet. Come in.'

She stepped in carefully; the house exhaled like it had been waiting for her, for this very moment. The door groaned loudly as it closed behind them, echoing through what felt like each bone of the estate. The air inside was strangely colder than outside.

The entrance hall stretched out in front of her, dark wood everywhere with gold trims. A long rug ran across the floor, faded red and brown. Paintings lined the walls everywhere, people in old clothes, their eyes seemingly following her around. There were no windows open, but it still smelled like smoke and something nostalgic like dusty books, wax, and faint lavender. Janet moved fast. Eliza walked quickly to keep up, this did not help her lungs either which still felt extremely tight.

Janet hastily spoke. 'You will be in west wing. Meals are with Miss Clara unless told otherwise. Breakfast at eight.'

'Is… Miss Clara well?' Eliza asked hesitantly.

Janet shrugged. "You will see."

They walked through two hallways and up a flight of old creaky stairs. The farther they went, the more the house changed. The walls looked older, the floors squeaked more. Wallpaper was peeling like the house was trying to shed its own skin. They stopped abruptly at a door.

'Here,' Janet firmly spoke, pushing it open.

The room was small but clean. A single bed, a desk, and a narrow wardrobe. A shiny metal pitcher sat on a stand near the window. Someone had lit a small fire, but it did not do much. On the desk sat a yellow lit candle. Its glow made the shadows on the walls move as if she was not the only one staying in this room.

'I will come back soon. The family will want to meet you.'

And then she was gone. No noise.

Eliza stepped in setting her bag on top of the neatly made bed. She glanced out the window. Beyond the gardens, there were woods that looked like they went on for miles, their trees so close together it seemed as if there was no air to breathe. She opened her satchel, two books… one story, one Latin. Her silver pendant ice cold from the journey. A pair of gloves.

And the letter that started all this. She put these items in designated places around *her* room, nice and organised.

She pulled her hair out of the loose braid and brushed it gently through with her fingers, tying it into a neat bun with her ribbon. Her reflection in the mirror was pale and tired. She did not look like a governess; she looked like a little girl trying not to be afraid of a new mysterious place.

Somewhere downstairs a bell rang loud.

She stood still for a moment, holding her breath. Too scared to move an inch while she figured out what it was, where it came from and what it was for. She soon realised that the bell may just be the noise that is meant to get Eliza and Clara to come down to see the family, though she was still unsure. Janet had not informed her of this bell.

The fire in her room crackled, the candle flickered and the estate whispered. Of course, not with words but with presence and feeling.

Eliza smoothed her skirt once again and reached for her gloves. Then she opened the solid oak door and stepped into the silence. The bell had stopped and the corridors looked different.

Chapter Four

The Harrows

The corridor did not look the same as before when Janet had shown her around.

Eliza stood still, one hand resting on the wooden pillared banister and the other by her side. She stared down the length of the hallway she had to walk down. She could have sworn… no, she knew, the floor was different before. Earlier when she arrived it was something like raw wood, creaking with every step and floorboards wobbly, but now it was carpeted in a pale green shade and a bit threadbare at the edges, though carpeted, nonetheless.

The soft grey light coming through the hallway window cast subtle shadows on the faded wallpaper which she did not recognise either. There had been a tear near the corner, she remembered it clearly, and a brown stain that looked like an old handprint. Both were gone. In their place hung paintings. Still life. Bruised rotting pears and plums spilling out of a cracked etched flower porcelain bowl, the background an ash colour, as if someone smudged graphite. It had not been there earlier.

Eliza did not speak; she only blinked slowly and walked forward holding her breath unintentionally. Her socks sank softly into the rug with every step she took. Maybe she had remembered it wrong, they were walking quickly earlier after all. Maybe the house had always looked like this. Maybe she was tired from the long journey. Her fingers brushed the wall as she passed, half expecting it to change right there and then. But it did not.

Downstairs, footsteps moved heavily on the creaky floorboards. The clink of silver and mutters of voices echoed throughout the once silent estate. She followed the sound, the air becoming colder the closer she came to the great hall. The soft peach hair on her body stood guard.

Janet was waiting. Again. She gave Eliza a sharp look that told her to stand straight and say nothing foolish. Janet's hair was pulled even tighter than when Eliza first met her; her black apron dirtied with white like Eliza's mothers was.

'This way,' she said flatly, and turned.

They passed another corridor, no… the same corridor surely, but now lined with different portraits. Different people. Eliza's stomach tightened, she did not ask. She did not want an answer really.

They entered the drawing room.

A high-ceilinged room with deep green walls and tall shuttered windows. A fireplace in the centre roared with fresh coal and the thick scent of smoke hung in the air. The furniture was carefully arranged: symmetrical, tidy, untouched. Chairs that looked sat in more by ghosts than guests, a writing desk by the window with a closed ink bottle and curtains thick enough to block the entire world out.

Lady Imogene Harrow stood near the fireplace. Her grey silk gown clung tightly to her arms, and her pale blonde hair was twisted neatly into a bun. She looked younger than Eliza expected, like porcelain but with a hint of tiredness.

'Miss… Fe…Fell.' Her voice stuttered. 'You… you are on time.'

'Yes, my lady.' Eliza curtsied low.

'You will begin your duties tomorrow. Breakfast commences at eight, lessons at eight thirty and concludes at five with intervals for meals and prayer. Clara requires close attention. You shall speak to the steward about scheduling.'

'Yes, my lady.'

Only then did Eliza glance around the room again. There curled in a red velvet chair sat Clara. Eliza's first thought was how small she seemed, not physically but in presence. A muted red coloured dress buttoned to the neck, pale skin, colourless hair in loose braids and hands folded gently in her lap. Her eyes flicked up and met Eliza's, then flicked away just as fast. It was not shyness, it was caution. The kind you saw in foxes or deer before they bolt.

Clara gave her a small smile. She smiled like it cost her.

Lord Harrow remained seated in an armchair by the window. Eliza had not noticed him until then. He was in the dark with shadows covering most of his face, he did not speak. He just watched her or through her, she could not tell.

The walls felt closer than before… again.

Dinner was served in the great hall, it is a long room with high ceilings and way too many candles. The table stretched father than necessary, its only purpose was to fill the room space, set with polished silver and plates patterned in golden leaves around the edges. It all glistened under the low chandeliers perfectly even though everything felt slightly… off? Just the smallest bit. Eliza could not quite name it.

The family sat in assigned places, as though choreographed: Lady Imogene at the head, Lord Harrow opposite.

Eliza was placed two seats from Clara who did not speak throughout, dabbing politely at her food. On the table was soup, warm bread rolls, and roasted lamb, but Eliza barely tried any of it. Her hands shook slightly each time she reached for her cutlery.

Lady Imogene asked her about her previous studies. Eliza answered politely. Parish school, lessons from the vicar, borrowed books read all the time. She did not mention how many nights she had taught herself Latin by copying phrases in a torn notebook until her fingers cramped up.

'Do you read poetry?' The Lady asked inquisitively.

'Yes, my lady. Blake… Wordsworth, sometimes.'

'Good.' Imogene replied sternly. 'Clara must recite Dawnton without fail by March.'

Clara looked down at her plate. Silence followed loudly.

Lord Harrow finally spoke near the end of the meal, his voice was quiet but meaningful.

'You will find the estate quiet, Miss Fell.'

Eliza nodded but said nothing.

'They say silence sharpens the mind. That is why I have remained here all these years.'

She glanced at Clara who still had not spoken.

They said he rarely left the estate and now she knew why. The walls were his world, the Lady, Clara, now Eliza were just sounds inside it like dolls in a dollhouse.

Later, in her room, Eliza lit a candle and tried to write a letter. She sat at the small desk, hands cold, thoughts scattered.

> *Dear Mother,*
> *I've arrived safely. The house is huge and very old. The family keeps to themselves a lot. My room is warm enough and Clara seems quiet but sweet. I am still unsure what to think of it all, but I'm here for work and I'll do it well...*

She paused.

She had not lied, not exactly. But she cannot forget the way Lord Harrow looked at her and the way the corridor changed each time she walked through it like the house was testing her memory. She folded the letter up instead of sealing it. Instead, she stood by the window to look out. The gardens below were silent and still. Frost coated the grass like broken glass on concrete, the trees stood tall after the gusts of wind earlier showing is strength and power. But near the edge of the gardens by the woods, there was someone. A boy. Young and looked as if he was dressed in brown dungarees, or it was dirty.

He had a rake in his hand shovelling frost and leaves. He paused only once to look up, and it was right at her. They locked eyes, her breath stopped unintentionally. She also realised that he was actually a man and looked to be in his mid to late twenties. Then, he vanished just like that into the trees. She leaned forward heart pounding. The candle flickered violently behind her matching her heartbeat.

She did not sleep much that night, every creak of floorboard sounded like a footstep, every flick of a shadow seemed alive. The house was changing, she was sure of it. Rearranging itself slowly like a creature luring its prey and somehow, she was invited into its mouth.

Chapter Five

She Was Not the First, and Would Not Be the Last

Eliza had always liked quiet. It had been something steady and familiar to her, something she could rest inside. But at Greywick, the silence was different, it felt heavy and at times, oppressive and there was little relief from it. It also felt as though it was always listening too.

The house seemed to pause between sounds, holding its breath like it knew something that she did not. The clocks ticked very slowly, dragging each second out on purpose. The corridors felt longer than before and stretched way farther out in ways that made her question her own sense of sanity and directions. Even the windows made it hard for her, stiff and stubborn as if they had not been opened properly in years. Sealed shut, maybe for a reason maybe not.

She had been tutoring Clara for six days. Or maybe seven. It was hard to tell. The days blended together here like water poured to the rim of a glass; it eventually just looks empty. Each morning followed the same pattern. Weak tea on a tray. The distant ticks of the grandfather clock in the hallway by the door.

Clara waiting by the window with her hands folded neatly in her lap, already seated when Eliza arrived.

Clara did not fight the lessons and that was what unsettled Eliza the most. There was no boredom, no irritation, no rebellion. She met Latin with a mild interest, though Clara's attention waned halfway through some of the sentences. Piano lessons had a lot of long pauses, fingers shaking hovering over the keys as if she had forgotten what she had just 'learnt.' Reading brought questions that began very well and engaging. She had a lot of questions and wanted to learn more but soon enough after some time the attention faded before they were finished.

Needlework was the most difficult for sure. Clara's fingers kept getting tangled in the thread, knots forming everywhere where clean, neat, pretty stitches should have been. Eliza corrected her at first by undoing the mistakes and showing her how to guide the needle properly. She even slowed it down for her, but Clara only smiled at the errors; she never tried to fix them herself. It was as if the process mattered more than the outcome for almost everything. This was very interesting to Eliza because she found back at home tutoring in the Parish school that they would hate the process but enjoy the positive outcome. Clara was very different in that sense.

One afternoon, Eliza leaned over Clara's shoulder and noticed she was drawing instead of practising her letters Eliza told her to do.

The half scrunched up piece of paper was filled with the same shape, repeated again and again. It was not writing. Not a picture. But a spiral. Very balanced, even, and deliberate.

Perfect in a way that made Eliza think it was from her memory rather than imagination.

'What's that?' Eliza asked.

Clara did not look up. 'It's just something I remember,' she said quietly. 'It's always been here.'

She did not say where 'here' was. Eliza did not ask.

The only place Eliza felt the air properly was outside, inside was always stuffy and very trapped and contained with what felt like almost no air at all. When lessons ended and it was still daylight she would walk around the grounds. The estate was large and quite poorly kept, brambles and hedges growing wild and unchecked. They were curling around the land like a snake strangling its prey. The paths were uneven and almost non-existent, eaten up by all of the weeds that stood brave. It was during one of these walks that she saw the man again. The same one from her window.

He was quite lean with his skin worn from the sun and dirt beneath his fingernails. His boots were almost dead, his sleeves rolled up as he trimmed the hedges carefully, methodical in his movements to make sure it was perfect to the Lord and Lady's place. He did not look up; he was so focused and ingrained in what he was doing until she stepped on a twig that made a bit of a snap.

'Didn't hear ya Comin',' he said.

'I didn't mean to sneak,' Eliza replied. 'Sorry. Do you work here?'

He nodded. 'Most days. Isaac Turner.' He put out his right hand

'Eliza Fell. Tutor.' She put out her left hand, and they shook, then stopped and both pulled back their hands.

He paused for, well…long enough. 'You're not the first, ya know.'

She blinked. 'Pardon?'

'To tutor her,' he said, gesturing his hand and body vaguely toward the house. 'Clara. You're not the first. Won't be the last.'

Before Eliza could respond, he returned to his work as if the conversation were finished. She was stunned by his blatant rudeness but could not think of a suitable response so she returned to her room.

That evening she said nothing or anything at dinner. There was little conversation anyway. Meals at Greywick felt formal and hollow, polite in a way that discouraged people to speak. Lady Imogene sat rigid, her wine barely touched. Lord Harrow murmured a few estate related matter to his wife, but that was all.

Clara ate quietly, as if trying not to be noticed at all.

Only the cutlery made noise.

Later in the week, Eliza wandered toward the edge of the estate's grounds near the woods, stopping just before the trees grew thick and the view darkened. That was when she noticed it. A small clearing of trees and bushes which was slightly hidden. Six names were carved deeply and meaningfully into a dry bit of bark on a tree. Different handwriting. Different depths. All first names. All women. The dates made her stomach tighten a little. They were out of order and overlapping. One name had been scratched out in a line, as if someone had tried to get rid of it.

Did they leave the estate or were they never been allowed to? Were they hated?

Eliza had so many questions bombarding her head.

That night the wind battered the house, rattled all the windows and it forced its way through every nook and cranny into the house. Eliza wrapped herself up tightly in her quilt because the fire had burned out from the heavy wind pushing through.

She tried to write to home again, but none of the words in the English language could ever convey her thoughts and feeling to her family in any meaningful way, so she gave up. She just did not know what to say. That Clara drew symbols repetitively and she did not know what it represented or tell you what it was. That the corridors change every time she walks down them though the same direction always leads to the same rooms. Or that her name, Eliza, might one day end up carved into the same tree as the others and it worried her. They would think she had gone mad.

She carefully folded the unfinished letter and regarded the slightly crinkled paper before placing it in her bedside oak wood drawer that squeaks. She turned to her yellow faintly smelling candle that still stood strong against the wind, blew up her cheeks and poof. She blew out the candle, but… she heard it. Not a normal smoke rising quickly sound, but a sound from somewhere in the room she did not know. Behind the wall. Above the ceiling. Beneath the floor. It sounded like laughter. Or crying. Definitely was not the candle making that noise.

'Something was always just out of sight,' she whispered to herself. 'A whisper behind the door, a shadow in the mirror.'

She pulled the covers tighter and closed her eyes tightly.

Chapter Six

Ashes

It was raining again. Typical.

It did not fall or tip but trickled slowly, seeping deep into the bones of the house warping the outside view into blurred darkness. Eliza sat at her desk, the black ink drying on the page slowly as she ponders of what to write next. She had rewritten the letter three times now, each draft is a lot shorter than the previous one.

"Dear Samuel…"

Her brother would not understand this place, not with everything that has been happening. She put the cap back on the ink bottle and laid the pen down. This time she would finish the letter. The letter was not long, but it had every single detail inside. She sealed it with some red fancy wax pressed gently into the envelope, securing it in place. Just like the one she got to come here. Janet was sweeping the hallway when Eliza hesitantly stepped out with the letter in hand.

'Would you…' Eliza began, unsure why she felt like she was sending off something bad inside. 'Would you deliver this please? When you next go to town.'

Janet did not take it at first. She glanced up and down the corridor then back at Eliza. Her hands reached out for the letter quickly, snatching it as if it were banned.

'I will do my best,' she replied quietly, slipping the letter into her apron pocket. 'But nothing posted from here ever stays posted for long.'

Eliza furrowed her eyebrows inquisitively. 'Wha… what do you mean?'

Janet shook her head. 'You cannot fix a house built on lies, Miss Fell. It will crumble eventually and take you with it.'

Later on, in the night Eliza walked past the fireplace in the east corridor.

Ash.

Leftovers of black burnt torn paper with faint red wax hardened on one of the edges. She knelt down, heart pounding and sifted through the dusty, crumbling mess. Fingers shaking. Janet had not even left the house, and someone made sure Eliza's words never would. One inch of paper survived, and it had Eliza's handwriting on it. She was sure it was her letter she wrote.

The air inside Greywick disappeared after that.

Eliza noticed how people appeared around her without any sound and how conversations always seemed to end the minute she walked into the room. She began watching the staff closely. There were few, most stayed silent and distant, but one man stood out. She had never seen him before, but he knew her name. She had taken a wrong turn, not far… just past the linen cupboards on the second floor trying to get to the library, onto a hallway she did not recognise. A door at the end was slightly open. She creeped over, towards it.

'Miss Fell.'

The voice came from behind. Calm. She turned and it was a tall man in a butler's coat with black gloved hands.

'I… I am very sorry,' she stuttered, stepping back. 'I was trying to…'

'This wing is not for guests,' he interrupted. 'It is undergoing repair.'

She hesitated. 'And you are?'

'I have always been here,' he replied quickly. 'Although, I am not often seen.'

He gave no name. Just turned and walked the other way, his steps making no noise.

Clara started to randomly appear in doorways with no warning. She moved around the house silently and strategically as if she were a piece on a chessboard.

'You had a rattle when you were a baby, yes?' She asked one morning as Eliza was setting up Latin class.

Eliza looked up confused. 'I don't… I don't know.'

Clara tilted her head slightly. 'I think you did. It had a bright golden star on the handle. I liked it.'

'You *think* I did?'

Clara nodded. 'Yes!'

Eliza stared at her wondering where this conversation would lead and why it even started. 'Why would you know that?'

'I remember,' Clara stated. 'From when we were small.'

'We were not small together, Clara. Besides, I am older than you!'

'We were not?'

She smiled softly but absently, like the question did not mean anything at all. She smiled like it cost her. Later, in the garden, Eliza found Isaac. He was knee-deep in soil, trying to bring the frosted roses back to life. His hands were muddy to his elbows, his shirt covered, he did not look up when she headed over to him - like always. He kept digging and trimming away, so focused on his job to make it as perfect as possible for the Lord and Lady.

'Did you know,' Eliza muttered, 'that the letters may never leave this place?'

Isaac gave a grunt, continuing with his job.

'And the butler, do you know his name? The one who watches east wing?'

Isaac glanced up at those questions showing his confused look on his face.

'There's no butler.'

Eliza was confused and felt a rush of coldness through her body leaving her covered with goosebumps.

'I saw him,' she insisted. 'He stopped me.'

Isaac stood up slowly, dusting off his hands. He was less confused now, more intrigued but serious about it.

'Don't dig too far, Miss Fell.'

'Why?' She questioned without hesitation

He looked back at the house standing tall against the smoky coloured sky.

'Because this place eats its own.'

That night the door to east wing made a noise echoing throughout the halls. Just once. Like someone had slammed it. Eliza did not open her door, she just sat upright in the solid bed clutching at her quilt, staring at the doorknob. It stopped, but the laughter did not. This time it was louder, and it sounded like it came from inside the walls.

Chapter Seven

Winter Eyes

February 1816

The piano was much colder than it had looked. Eliza's fingertips hovered over the keys, holding her breath as her skin brushed the ivory smoothed by time and use. She played a note, fingers trembling. It echoed across the drawing room disappearing into the stillness and quietness of the house. The sky outside was thick with mist like it always was, it left the corners of the windows wet with condensation that kept growing as it got mistier and colder.

The afternoon light was a little brighter and spilled in through the thin linen curtains leaving patches of shadow playing across the room which gave a kind of calmness to Eliza. She pressed another key, then another. A song began to form in her, familiar yet just out of reach in her memory. She could not quite put a name to the song she was playing but the notes floated around the room like dust particles; sounds made of half memory. Behind her, Clara sat on a footstool, legs tucked underneath her like a doll carefully positioned. She watched out of the window, her colourless hair unbraided for the first time since Eliza got to the estate. Clara then began to hum low and gently, perfectly in tune with what Eliza was playing.

Eliza's hands froze mid-chord.

'You know this?' She questioned.

Clara turned her head away from the window, now looking at Eliza. 'I think I do.'

'But I have never played it before on the piano.'

Claras face wrinkled in concentration briefly, then her shoulders followed into their familiar form as a shrug. 'Maybe someone else did.' She smiled awkwardly. 'Or maybe you forgot?'

Just then the door creaked open. Lady Imogene stood in the doorway, her pale hand still resting on the door handle. Her eyes traced the room, then focused on Eliza, Clara and the piano.

'You are blessed with delicate hands, Miss Fell.' She observed with admiration. 'It seems the piano has taken quite a liking to you.'

'I… thank you,' Eliza tripped over her words, unsure of how to respond.

Lady Imogene stepped into the room, her slippers making no sound against the floor as if she were floating. She did not approach, she simply stood and observed.

Eliza glanced down at the keys again, unsure whether to keep playing. Clara started humming again so Eliza followed on the piano. Lady Imogene turned around abruptly.

'Excuse me,' she snapped.

She left suddenly. No explanation, no goodbye.

Shortly after, Clara went to her room and Eliza found herself alone in the music room. The fire had died down to just few glowing embers. She wandered around the room slowly, trailing her fingers idly across the furniture until she returned to the patiently waiting piano. She noticed that the piano stool she had been seated on had a lid. She opened it and was delighted to find some sheet music and a book. Her hand touched something sharp, it left a small cut on her index finger. A corner of some loose pages sticking out from the music sheets. She looked thoroughly through the pages until she found the offending loose pages, however, it was not about music like the rest of the book. The pages were browned at the edges, ink slightly smudged, tucked away with care as if it were hidden and not lost. She opened it.

> *'She has eyes like winter rain. Cold. Too knowing for someone so small… I worry what she sees, what she already understands. The mirror knows. And still, I loved her way before she had a name.'*

The words made goosebumps all over Eliza. Signed beneath it: M.F. Her fingers shook.

'Margaret Fell?' She whispered under her heavy breaths.

Her mother had never written like this, well… not that Eliza had ever seen. She read it again.

'Before she had a name.'

Was this about her? She folded it carefully and tucked it into the inside pocket of her linen dress. Eliza glanced towards the piano and caught her reflection in the mirror above. Only, it did not feel like her reflection. The girl in the mirror had her shape, her pale skin, her icy eyes, however, something about it did not seem like her. She looked away.

That night Eliza laid under the quilt, candle blown out, letter hidden under her soft pillow. The room was quiet and still, though her thoughts were anything but. She was kept awake wondering too much. She was still baffled as to why Lady Imogene had dashed off from the music room, of Clara humming along with the tune Eliza was playing, yet she herself did not know how she knew it, and of the words carefully laid out on a note hidden away.

A name popped into her mind: Lissy. It was like a whisper. She had never been called that as far as she was aware, not by Samuel or her mother. It felt familiar but she did not know why.

A soft knock shook through the wooden door, she held her breath, but no one entered. Then footsteps, slow and deliberate, paced outside her door. A shadow formed beneath the crack of the door. She did not move.

When the shadow and noises left, she crept over to her window and opened the shutters just enough to let the cool night air inside. The trees had gathered mist around their branches like dressing gowns. She saw nothing else, though the house did not sleep. It listened.

Eliza held the pendant around her neck in her palm. The chain was cold and the locket held no photo. She went under her pillow to look at the old page again.

'The mirror knows.'

She glanced over her shoulder slowly. Her own reflection waiting in the wardrobe mirror, moved a second after she did.

Chapter Eight

Where Secrets Unfold

The snow had stopped by morning, but the estate still was silent. The cold did not just settle on the ground; it crept into the lungs and bones of everyone including the house. Eliza and Clara were walking down the corridor just after noon when the Lord and Lady were napping. Janet was in the kitchen, and the other servants seemed to vanish after lunch.

'That wing is off limits,' Eliza whispered glancing at the sturdy oak door at the corridor's furthest end. 'They said it is sealed for repairs.'

Clara's eyes gleamed mischievously. 'Which means it will be fun!'

Eliza hesitated but smiled indulgently, it felt good to be having fun and she was relieved that Clara was showing more than a polite interest in something. The corridor felt different, like it was silently listening in. But Clara was already tiptoeing ahead, her bare feet silent on the floorboards, dress floating. Eliza held her breath and followed.

The East Wing door creaked open. It was not locked. Inside, the air was musty, and everything was thick with dust.

White linen sheets were draped over furniture, and the windows were boarded up, barely letting any light in to the room.

'Stay close,' Eliza whispered again.

They crept around the room looking for something, something they did not even know they were looking for. There were white draped chairs, a cracked vanity table and a shelf half falling down. Broken children's toys covered the floor; cracked porcelain dolls, burnt books and a rattle half smashed with no beads inside.

Clara crouched beside the toys. 'Look,' she murmured. 'There is soot…'

Eliza swept the soot with her finger to get a closer look and smell. Clara dug around, lifting all the sheets slightly to see what was underneath.

'Eliza!' Clara whispered urgently attracting her attention.

A cradle was found next to the fireplace, undamaged and looking brand new. There was a silver nameplate nailed across the side with letters etched deeply.

Eliza.

Her body trembled, a slight sharp pain in her chest, like a small stone was lodged there. Footsteps. They both froze.

Quickly, Eliza grabbed Clara's hand and pulled her inside a wooden wardrobe. It was small but they both squeezed in, sucking their body inwards to make more room.

Through a gap in the wardrobe door, Eliza saw him… Lord Harrow. He entered the room like someone visiting a cemetery. Lord Harrow stood next to the cradle for a long time. Did not speak, did not touch it, just stared blankly. Then, with a deep sigh, he turned and left, closing the door behind him.

They did not move for a full minute just to make sure he was really gone, they were both breathing shallowly, all senses heightened waiting for a creak, a shadow, a smell, anything. They both looked at each other with agreement then opened the wardrobe door. Positive that he had really gone.

'He used to come in here a lot… when it was your room.' Clara spoke quietly.

Eliza was completely shocked, she whispered. 'What?'

But Clara was already wandering back to the rattle, her voice soft and quiet. 'I think this was yours, the rattle I told you about a while ago. Janet told me once, though she said she was not supposed to, but…'

Eliza grabbed her hand, cutting off Clara's sentence. 'We need to go.'

The next morning, she was woken up by Clara jumping on her bed.

'ELIZA, ELIZA, WAKE UP!'

'What's wrong, Clara? Has something happened?' Eliza nervously responded.

'No, no. It is my birthday!' She was gleaming with joy and happiness, something rarely seen.

Eliza wished her a happy birthday and got ready for the day, heading down for breakfast. It was Clara's fifteenth. The Lord and Lady were already downstairs in the breakfast room surrounded by delicious foods, presents and a vanilla sponge cake cut into eight symmetrical slices. Eliza nibbled at hers politely but left most of it still on the plate. No one noticed.

Later that day, Lord Harrow announced that a grand ball would be held at Greywick this coming weekend. An event to honour Clara and, as Lady Imogene added, 'to remind the neighbouring families that we are not to be forgotten.'

Invitations were made and sent out. The house had a strange feeling, like it was alive again. Rooms were scrubbed immaculately, silver candelabras polished, and fresh flowers brought in daily. Even the weather seemed to have brightened.

On the morning of the ball, Clara ran into Eliza's room holding a box with a butter yellow silk dress inside.

'Look! This one is mine. But you are coming too.'

Eliza stared. 'Me?'

'Yes. They said so. They want you to look… presentable. Janet is already warming the curling irons up.'

Eliza gulped, the thought of walking into that ballroom among strangers, rich pretentious strangers, made her panic. But she nodded.

The maids fussed over her in Clara's bedroom, curling her hair into waves and tying it with a velvet green ribbon. Light powder dusted across her face, making her look more ghostly than she already was, with a dab of ruby red tint across her lips.

"You look almost like a lady," Janet said with a wink.

Clara lent her a gown of her own, a deep ivy green taffeta dress with lace sleeves and the tiniest of pearls sewn into the bodice. It hung a little loose on Eliza, she had not been eating much lately. Eliza had begun to feel that meals were chores, not pleasures, mainly because of the palpable atmosphere around the table. But she felt lighter every day, empty, in a way that comforted her, and it was not a bad thing surely?

That evening the estate went from a rundown, haunted looking house, to a lively home with people, flowers, music, laughter and more. The grand hall was lit perfectly, the music played under the arches, and it no longer smelt like dust but of candles and fresh flowers.

Guests poured in, men with top hats and glass monocles, woman with laced hands and poised looks. Servants in black coats stood in perfectly lined rows. Introductions filled the room, followed by lots of chatter. Eliza stood and watched, a glass of cordial shaking in her hands, she was not hungry. The cakes lined up on polished silver trays made her feel sick just to look at.

'She was born from a secret,' someone had once said, or maybe it was a thought that formed as a voice, 'raised where no one knew and yet she walked into that house like she had a right to be there.' She felt it tonight, the weight of their eyes staring deeply into her soul and bones. Somewhere in the crowd, Lord Harrow was watching her.

As the waltz started and the room spun with dancers, Eliza slipped away toward the side corridor. Her breath caught in her throat, dress felt too tight, skin too pale. She needed air, she needed… space. Behind her, the music played on.

Chapter Nine

Beneath the Ivy, Beneath the Truth

Frost coated the estate grounds outside Eliza's window that morning. Even before she woke and got up, she felt its presence in the still air, the way the cold seeped in through the bricks and along the floorboards. Her breath created clouds as she leaned to unhook the latch of the window showing the frozen garden, ghostlike beneath the pale February sky. The trees, bare of leaves, stood tall.

She dressed slowly, choosing a faded wool dress that once belonged to Clara. It hung from her shoulders more than it had last month but she barely noticed. Her stomach twisted as she fastened the bodice, not from hunger but from something else. She had not eaten much since the ball for Clara's birthday. Food has started to make her feel slow and heavy, like she was losing something she had only just begun to grasp. Control maybe? Either way, she did not like it and so refused breakfast again.

Downstairs she met Isaac by the hedges, the ones where they had first met. He wore a battered coat and fingerless gloves, and his boots were wet with melted snow. He did not smile.

'You still want to see the old gardens?' he asked.

She nodded, wordless. Her heart was beating loudly in her ears.

They left the path quickly, crossing into a part of the estate where no one went anymore; not Clara, not the maids, not even the crows, it seemed. Branches grabbed her dress, brittle with frost. Ivy clung to every tree, strangling it tightly. Stone benches once pretty are now crumbling under the weight of time and weather. A statue of a weeping cherub had lost its face entirely.

'This place used to be something beautiful,' Isaac said as they passed the ruins of what might have once been a fountain. 'The gardeners kept it alive. All year round. The winter blooms were famous.'

'And now?' she whispered.

'Now it's a place people pretend doesn't exist.'

They kept walking deeper into the wild. She could feel the air was still, like it was holding its breath alongside Eliza. Finally, they reached a small clearing… so small.

It was tangled with vines so much that she almost missed it. In the middle of the clearing was single flat stone on the floor half swallowed by moss. It was cracked near the base.

Eliza knelt and brushed at the surface with her gloved hands, then she picked with her bare fingers where the frost was too deep into the carvings. The inscription carved into the stone made her freeze.

Margaret Fell

Faithful Lover. Devoted Mother.

1800

Eliza sat back so quickly she nearly fell. 'No,' she said aloud, voice shaking. 'That's not right. That can't be…'

Isaac watched her from the edge of the clearing. 'I thought it might be name you knew.'

'That's my mother's name,' she muttered. 'But… she's alive. She raised me. She…' Eliza shook her head. 'She's not dead.'

'She isn't,' Isaac agreed calmly. 'That stone's just for show. Far as I know no body was ever buried here. Grounds were never disturbed. It's just a marker.'

'Who put it here?' Eliza questioned with furrowed brows.

'Lord Harrow did. Back in 1800. Said it was for 'his grief,' but never talked of it. Told the gardeners to let ivy grow over it.'

'But… 1800?' Eliza repeated. 'That's the year I was born.'

Isaac nodded slowly. 'That's what makes it strange, don't it?'

She turned and walked back toward the house without another word. That night, after a silent supper she barely touched, Eliza returned to her room and lit a candle. The flame flickered, casting her reflection into a blur on the windowpane. Her hands shook as she unfolded some paper.

> *Dearest Mother,*
> *There is a grave on the grounds here, a grave with your name. Dated the year I was born. They say it is just a stone, that no one is beneath it. But why would he put it there? What is he hiding? What are you not telling me?*

She stopped. Eliza had done the maths and whilst she was not a worldly girl, she knew that pregnancy was nine months for humans, therefore her mother and Lady Imogene were pregnant at the same time! She stopped. The ink had smudged where her fingers were shaking. The words felt too loud, too honest. She crumpled the page, then smoothed it out again.

Her fingers moved to the floorboard beside her bed. She pried it up with careful fingers, revealing the small space beneath.

Four letters lay there already, all written, none sent. One of them had dried lavender tucked inside. She added this one to the pile, pressing it gently between the others.

The floorboard creaked as she replaced it. There were no answers yet. Only the letters. Only the feeling that every truth she uncovered went into a deeper mystery, like a never-ending cycle of finding the truth about the truth.

In the mirror above the fireplace, she saw herself. Pale cheeks with hollowed blue and purple beneath her eyes. The dress she wore now felt looser than it had last week. But she did not think of food, only of the grave. The name. The lies. Somewhere, beneath the floorboards of this house or inside its crumbling gardens, the real deep truth waited. She just had to survive long enough to find it.

She curled under her thin blanket, but her skin prickled. Sleep did not come easily anymore. When it did, it came in flashes. The sound of a rattle, the crack of glass, a woman's voice calling her name down the long corridors that no longer existed. Sometimes she woke with her fists clenched, nails digging into the bedsheet, teeth aching from how hard she had bitten down.

The next morning passed quickly and quietly. The household was unusually quiet. Lord and Lady Harrow had gone into town, Clara had a headache again and the corridors were empty, apart from the occasional sweeping of Janet's broom. Eliza sat at the small desk by the window and scribbled another letter, but this one was shorter. Less frantic.

You wouldn't lie to me. Would you?

She folded it carefully and pressed it flat. Her hands trembled less today but her wrists looked thinner under her sleeves. She skipped breakfast again, said she was not hungry. Janet gave her a long look and left the tray anyway. When Eliza opened her wardrobe to put her shoes away, she paused.

Tucked behind the stacks of winter clothes was a faded wooden box she had not noticed before. Inside were scraps of ribbon, bits of yellowed lace, and underneath them… a tiny silver locket. Her fingertips brushed over the front, it had an engraving: a W, winding like ivy. When she opened it, she expected to see a picture, but it was empty. She turned it over and noticed the hinge had been forced open before. Something had once been in here, something removed. She held it for a moment longer, then placed it on her windowsill.

The storm came that evening. Rain lashed harshly against the glass; thunder growled over the estate like an angry predator.

She lay awake and thought of the name etched into stone. Margaret Fell. Faithful Lover. Devoted Mother. But devoted to whom? And what had she been forced to leave behind? Eliza turned onto her side and wrapped herself tightly in her blanket.

Chapter Ten

Reflections

April 1816

April brought a strange sunlight that seemed to expose the flaws in everything, the cracking wallpaper, the worn floorboards, and the fake smiles.

Eliza stood in front of the tall mirror that leaned against the wall of her bedroom, the hem of her nightgown dragging around her feet. She gazed at her reflection without really seeing it. Her eyes were unfocused, watery, red rimmed from sleepless nights. Beneath them, purple shadows bruised her pale skin, and her collarbones jutted sharper. She placed a hand against the glass, fingertips barely brushing it, and that was when it happened.

The mirror did not just reflect this time, it moved. The outline of her body flickered, blurred, and for a moment, she was no longer fifteen, no longer in that dim room. She was a baby and was being held by someone in a lavender dress, the scent of lilacs and linen were soft and strong. Her tiny hand clutched a rattle. A lullaby hummed through the air, off-key.

Then the voice. 'Eliza Harrow. My beautiful Eliza Harrow.'

She blinked. Her breath fogged up the glass, and the vision broke. The mirror showed only her once more, thin, hollow-eyed, frightened. But her memory… her memory was correct. She remembered the lavender fabric brushing her cheek, the rattle, the sound of that name spoken. And she remembered being called that. Eliza Harrow. She did not understand how. How she could remember things from so early, from an age where most minds were blank slates. But she did. She remembered like other people dreamed.

Later that day, as the rain made slow trails down the windows, Lady Imogene appeared in Eliza's room unannounced, bearing a brush in one hand and an unreadable look in her eyes. Without a word, she sat behind Eliza and began to comb through her tangled hair. The brush moved gently for once, no yanks or cold scolding about "presentation" or "decency." It was more personal than that. Eliza sat stiffly, uncertain whether to lean into the touch or pull away.

'You have her hair,' Imogene softly said after a while, not quite bitter, not quite delicate. Her voice hovered somewhere between the two.

Eliza did not move, only her lips. 'Whose?'

'I hated that.' Her hand paused mid-stroke, then resumed. 'Long and thick and… wild.'

Eliza didn't speak. She waited for more, but none came. Imogene stood, dropped the brush onto the vanity, and left the room without so much as a glance backward.

Dinner that evening was late. The hall was candlelit and heavy with tension. Clara toyed with her fork. Lady Imogene drank her wine too fast. The fire crackled a little too loudly, its warmth failing to touch any of them. Then Lord Harrow arrived. He swept in like a shadow with shoes, rain on his shoulders and mud crusted on the hem of his coat. The servants scattered. He did not apologise for the delay. He never did. He simply sat and spoke… of philosophy, of determinism, of fate.

'Do we choose our lives?' he thought aloud. 'Or are they chosen for us before we even breathe?'

Eliza watched him, his eyes never quite looked at hers. He seemed to see through her, around her.

'Some daughters,' he added, whilst slicing through a piece of lamb, 'are better off unaware.'

The clatter of silverware followed. Clara had stood so abruptly that her chair tipped over and fell behind her with a loud echoing thud.

'She is more your daughter than I will ever be,' she spat, her voice trembling with anger. Her cheeks were flushed, her breathing quick. Then she threw a spoon at the table, it struck the wine glass and shattered it, before storming from the room.

Silence.

Eliza did not move or breathe. Lord Harrow finally looked at her, really looked at her, and something in his expression changed. Recognition. Regret. Rage. He looked at her like she reminded him of a past that he thought he had got rid of. Lady Imogene poured herself more wine, eyes fixed on the broken glass. Lord Harrow resumed eating. The moment passed like a storm cloud floating across the sun; slow and dark.

That night, Eliza paced her room barefoot, steps soundless on the cold wooden floor. Her stomach churned but not from hunger. Hunger had become a companion now. A bowl of stew

Janet had left on her tray remained untouched by the door. Eliza had glanced at it once, then pulled her shawl tighter and sat instead by the window, staring into the sky. The house was too quiet.

The lullaby was back, but only in her head. She pressed her fingers to her temples, wanting the memories to stop. The name, the grave, the mirror, Eliza Harrow.

She lit a candle and began to write again. The ink trembled slightly on the page as she wrote another letter to the woman she had called Mother.

But of course, she did not finish it. Not this time. Not yet.

Chapter Eleven

Where Secrets Set Fire to the Quiet

The house slept under a mist that clung to its windows like when you breathe on a cold window. Somewhere, a clock struck one. Eliza walked soundlessly across the landing, the candlelight bobbing and flickering simultaneously with her steps. Shadows danced across the panelled walls, painting the portraits of long-dead ancestors in flickering light. She knew the way now…the loud creak in the third stair, the groan of the floorboard by the grandfather clock. It was like the house taught her how to move without waking it.

She went into the library, heart beating louder than her footsteps. The door clicked shut behind her. The scent of paper and old leather filled her nostrils. Hundreds of books towered around her; stories trapped behind cracked spines. She ran her fingers along the shelf edges until she found the drawer Lady Imogene had once locked with a silver key. Though tonight it was unlocked, coincidence? Inside, carefully folded, was a letter. Yellowed and crumpled with time, sealed once but now loose at the edges. It was dated: February 1801. She unfolded it with trembling fingers.

> *"To the child I may never be brave enough to hand this to, I was young when I first arrived at Greywick, a maid with too much hope and not enough protection. He watched me with interest, like someone picking a flower they don't plan to keep. And yet, for a moment, I believed in love.*
>
> *Lord Harrow came to see you once, only once. He meant to kill you, but instead we made a bargain.*
>
> *I was paid to leave. To disappear. To never return.*
>
> *So, I fled to Godalming, found Thomas and I tried to build something safe around the shards of what Greywick left me.*
>
> *But if you ever return there, I fear the estate will kill you.*
>
> *— M.F."*

Eliza's hands shook faster now. Margaret Fell, her mother. Her real father, the Lord, had tried to kill her. Her mother had fled with her and now here Eliza was, in the place she was not supposed to go to.

A creak echoed, then again and again. She frantically stuffed the letter into her skirt pocket, blew out the candle, and crouched behind the velvet armchair near the fireplace. Barely breathing. Listening. The door creaked open, a soft step followed. Then silence. After a pause, whoever it was turned and left again, leaving Eliza in the room hiding. She stayed in the dark a long while after just to make sure the coast was really clear. Back in her bedroom, she tucked the letter under the floorboard she had recently discovered beneath her bedpost. It was a loose plank that clicked out like it had been used before.

The walls of Greywick had secrets in their bones. She was just beginning to understand how many of them belonged to her.

The next morning, Clara sat at the breakfast table sipping tea like she had not shattered the family the night before. Lady Imogene buttered toast with careful precision, her eyes never meeting Lord Harrow's. He read the newspaper in silence. Eliza toyed with her spoon, her appetite nonexistent. The eggs cooled untouched.

'You did not sleep,' Clara mentioned, not looking up.

Eliza replied hastily. 'Neither did you.'

Clara's mouth twitched. 'No. But I do not sneak about like a ghost.'

Eliza's hand froze on her teacup. 'I was not…'

Clara shrugged, cutting her off. 'You think I do not hear the floors creak? I know which steps make the least noise.'

Eliza wanted to ask her what she knew but Clara only smirked into her cup and said nothing more. Later on, Clara cornered her in the corridor between the music room and the greenhouse.

'You are trying to dig up things that were meant to stay buried,' she said sharply.

Eliza did not answer.

'You cannot steal a place in this family,' Clara continued. 'You either belong here or not.'

Eliza looked her in the eye. 'Then maybe I never wanted to belong.'

Clara opened her mouth to respond but footsteps echoed down the corridor, she walked away instead.

They both stayed in their rooms util the evening where the family dined in the green drawing room. Lamps glowed. Tables dressed perfectly. Lord Harrow arrived late, his coat soaked with rain and his presence was as heavy as smog. His boots left damp prints across the rug as he handed his coat to a waiting footman and moved silently to his seat. Dinner was roast duck with glazed sweet potatoes and purple carrots. Eliza's plate remained almost untouched again.

Lord Harrow did not look up as he spoke. 'You should eat.'

'I am not hungry,' she replied, her voice steady.

Lady Imogene dabbed her lips with a linen napkin. 'Then at least pretend,' she added softly. 'It keeps the peace.'

Clara gave a soft laugh, sharp as glass. 'Peace? Is that what we are calling this now?'

No one answered her. The only sounds were the clink of cutlery, the gentle ticking of the mantle clock, and the occasional thunder rumbling outside.

Lord Harrow set his knife down hard and loud. 'Some in this house forget their place, they go looking where they should not. They open what was meant to stay closed.'

Clara's eyes flicked to Eliza, who kept hers fixed on the edge of her plate.

'She wants to know where she comes from,' Clara said. 'It is pathetic, really. Like digging through ash and hoping to find a whole photograph.'

Eliza quickly looked at Clara. 'Maybe it is better than pretending nothing ever burned.'

Lady Imogene poured herself more wine. 'The past is a heavy coat,' she said quietly. 'Wear it too long, and it shapes your body.'

Eliza stood up. The scrape of her chair against the rug felt louder than the thunder happening outside.

'Excuse me, I am tired.' No one stopped her.

In her bedroom, she knelt and lifted the loose floorboard again. The letter was still there, folded tight. She should burn it but that is not what she did, instead she placed it inside a hollowed book on her shelf: A Collection of English Ghost Stories, ironic enough to feel safe. She sat on the bed, candlelight flickering on the walls. The wind battered loudly on the windows; rain was heavier than before.

A knock. Eliza did not move, however no voice followed… just the knock. She stood slowly, opening the door but the hallway was empty. As she was closing the door something on the carpet, just outside her room, caught her eyes. It was a single purple carrot cold from dinner. She picked it up assuming it was a joke, though underneath it laid a scrap of paper.

Six words, written in urgent handwriting:

"You are not safe at night."

Chapter Twelve

A Season with Eyes

May 1816

Clara did not attend her Latin lesson that morning, nor embroidery, nor piano. When Clara crept past the classroom, she noticed Eliza pacing around the front of the room, as if she were teaching to an audience of ghosts.

'Clara has a headache,' Lady Imogene had said at breakfast. 'It is highly common in girls who are sensitive.'

Eliza had nodded, though Clara had never once come across to her as sensitive.

By the afternoon, the endless rain that had poured on the house for weeks was finally gone and a pale golden sunlight peeked its way into the hallways of the estate. Somewhere outside, the hedge maze dripped with the storm's tears, well… so did most of the garden.

Eliza felt restless. Her thoughts kept darting back to the letter under her floorboard, to the way Clara had looked at her during breakfast, and further back still, to her mother's final line.

If you ever return there, I fear the estate will kill you.

Greywick did not need poison or knives to hurt someone. It could do it with silence and it does.

When most of the house had settled, Eliza pushed open Clara's door. The curtains were drawn and a pale light peered through the ivy outside the windows. The room smelled of candle wax and lavender, but very faintly was there a smell… a smell like something other than a candle burnt.

The bed was not made. On the floor beside it, half-kicked under the rug, Eliza noticed something black and ashy. She bent down to look at what it was whilst her heart was pounding telling her not to. It was a paper doll. The kind children cut out from scrap materials with a blunt knife, but this one had been burnt. Across its chest in faint pencil was a name:

Eliza.

Behind her, the mattress rustled. Clara was lying on top of it still in her nightdress.

'You should not be in here,' Clara murmured.

Eliza held up the doll. 'Is this yours?'

Clara sat up slowly, her hair fell in messy knots. 'It used to be.'

'Why burn it?'

Clara smiled faintly. 'I wanted to see if ghosts could feel pain.'

Eliza frowned. 'What does that mean?'

Clara swung her legs over the edge of the bed. 'I had a sister once. She was taken to town. She had a cold, or so they said, and the doctors could not fix it. She never came back.'

Clara reached for the doll and turned it over in her hands. 'They told me she died.'

Eliza's breath caught. 'Clara…'

Clara's eyes met Elizas sharply. 'I thought it was a dream for years, that she was not real. But now I know that she did not die. They just replaced her.'

'Eliza?' she asked, though it sounded less like a name and more like an interrogation. 'Is that who you are now?'

Eliza did not answer.

Clara stood frantically and yelled. 'So, tell me… are you her? Or are you dead?'

Before Eliza could even respond, Clara pushed past and stormed out of the room. Eliza stood frozen in time for a moment trying to figure out what just happened, she hesitated then left the room to go back to her bedroom. Though halfway to her bedroom she was called down for who knows what. It was Lord Harrow. He called from the vestibule by the conservatory. The light outside had turned honey-gold, coating the estate in warmth. Eliza walked through and had paused by the ledge of roses, mesmerised by how suddenly everything had bloomed around here.

'You remind me of someone,' Lord Harrow said behind her. She turned to find him holding a small velvet box.

She did not take it.

He opened it anyway. Inside was a delicate pendant, pale opal with silver holding it in place, held by a thin but dainty chain.

'It belonged to your grandmother. You should have it.'

Eliza folded her arms. 'Why?'

'Because you are mine,' he said simply.

'No,' she replied sternly. 'I am my mother's.'

A muscle twitched in Lord Harrow's face. 'You do not understand what this place requires. What it costs to keep this the way it is.' He points around the room and through the window at the estates grounds.

'I think I do,' she battled, body burning up with rage.

He showed the box again, his tone gentle… too gentle. 'It is not a bribe; it is a gesture.'

'And this,' she said, taking a slow but meaningful step back, 'is a refusal.'

She turned effortlessly and walked away, leaving him and the opal pendant alone with nothing but shock to feel. In that moment Eliza felt powerful, she felt in control and craving more of it. She had become addicted to what she has not had in so long… the control, the power, the strength

Eliza could not sleep well that night, her eyes widened with the craving to do more, say more. She tossed and turned until the morning. It had arrived slowly, but it was worthwhile. The birds chirping to songs she does not know and the blossoms floating with elegance. The garden had come alive again. The estate was bright with green and faint yellows. A butterfly danced across her windowsill. Even the house seemed real peace for a second, like it was breathing and drinking in the beautiful new surroundings.

Eliza got dressed slowly and walked down to the edge of the garden. It had changed overnight, ripe with colour and warm with light. But something in all of this did not sit right with her, like it had changed too fast, too suddenly. She caught her reflection in the long glass-stained panes of the greenhouse windows. She was smiling but Eliza herself was not… her mouth had not moved. Behind her, the wind blew the flowers. But no one stood there, only in her reflection. Eliza's skin raised with bumps all over. Something in the house was watching her. Maybe it always had.

Chapter Thirteen

The Portrait Room

There were so many rooms in Greywick that you were frequently told that you were not allowed to go in, that Eliza has explored most of them except one. Some were sealed shut with rusted silver locks, others sealed with fear. This one had both.

Eliza had noticed it before, a small oak door at the end of the third-floor corridor, always shut. The keyhole was carved like an eye, as if each time she passed it, it watched her. Though this morning, something in her knew that she must enter to know what secrets it contained. She just had an intuition there was something important in that room which was compelling her onwards. The sun had barely woken up, and the corridor was a grey-blue tint, yet Eliza was up already.

She crept barefoot in her laced floral nightgown past the upstairs nursery and the servants' quarters, heart thudding like a knock in her chest… or on the door. The key was already in the lock, she did not know who had left it, perhaps it had always been there? With a faint click, the door opened sighing quietly with relief… or fear. A rush of cold musty air hit her face brutally, dust living in every crevice and on every surface of the room. The room kept the smell of neglect, dust, varnish, mildew, and death in a sour melange that it had managed to contain within its own walls which was fortunate as that meant everywhere else was bearable.

The room was narrow, it had ruby red velvet-draped furniture and frames with portraits of men and women in collars, lace gowns, riding coats, cravats and more. The Harrows, generation after generation hung in a row. Their faces varied…some proud, others rather depressed, but their eyes all had that same strange feeling. She moved down the line slowly, a man with prominent facial features and a scar on this left cheek, a pale woman in a forest-green gown holding a greyhound by leash, a young boy with a sad look as if he knows too much for his age, and then near the end slightly crooked on the wall was a portrait smaller than the others. It was a baby. The paintwork was delicate; you could tell someone had taken care with this one. The plaque beneath said:

"Eliza Harrow

Born 21 October 1800"

She had to remind herself to take a breath. It was her name, her birthday, herself in the portrait. But her mother had never painted her. Had she?

Eliza collapsed to the floor. It was not dramatic, not like in the theatres…it was simple, her bones and body forgot how to stand just like her lungs had forgot how to breathe. She heard the door creak; footsteps entered the room. Then a faint but recognisable voice.

'I wondered how long it would take.'

Janet.

Eliza looked up slowly. Her mouth worked, but no sound came out. Finally, in a cracked voice, she whispered, 'Why didn't anyone tell me?'

Janet crouched beside her, not touching her, not rushing. Just there.

'Because some names,' she said, looking at all the portraits sourly, 'come with bindings. Heavy ones. Ones that wrap around your neck and your whole future. And you were finally free of them.'

Eliza shook her head, tears trailing slowly down her cheeks. 'But I was not. I have always been here. Always been hers. Why keep me in the dark?'

Janet's voice was softer than before. 'Because Maggie gave up everything to break the chain. To keep you Eliza and not Harrow. Because she feared this house would take you back if it ever knew.'

Eliza looked at her mother's face in the portrait. She did not look afraid. She looked determined. Defiant.

'I was born here,' Eliza murmured.

Janet nodded.

'And he…he's my…'

'He is not your father,' Janet cut in, firmly but not unkindly. 'He is a man who has similar blood but nothing more than that. Your mother gave you everything else.'

Eliza swallowed. 'She said Greywick would kill me if I returned.'

Janet rose and stepped close to the window. 'It almost did. It still might. This house is not made for the living. It remembers too much. And now… so do you.'

Eliza stared at the portraits. At herself. At her mother. At the name she now carried like a crack across the mirror of her life.

Eliza Harrow.

Every part of her wanted to rip it off, to claw it away and be just Eliza again. Eliza from nowhere, daughter of Maggie, girl without a history.

But some truths refuse to stay buried.

She wiped her face and stood, legs shaking.

Janet turned and questioned. 'Now that you know, what will you do?'

Eliza stared at the child in the painting, the version of her that had never spoken, never walked, never remembered, and whispered, 'I'll find out what else they lied about.'

Janet did not smile, but there was a slight difference in her face and manner, like a silent approval. 'Then you should better start soon. Spring never lasts long here.'

Outside, a gust of wind pressed against the glass like a pent-up breath. The garden beyond the window moved like something waking.

The house had its eyes open again. Or so it felt.

Chapter Fourteen

All is Quiet

For days, the house was quiet, but not a normal nothing-to-say quiet, the one where you think you are being alienated, ignored or that someone knows a secret. Eliza barely spoke to anyone apart from during tutoring hours and even then, her voice was softer, quieter. Clara had started calling her 'Lissy.' The first time she said it Eliza thought it was a mistake or mishearing but then she said it again, and again and again, until it became the only name she would use. Every time it was used, Eliza's stomach churned. It always felt so familiar yet not remembered.

One morning, Janet brought her tea. She did not look at Eliza at all, and she was moving around much slower like she was creeping.

'Drink up!' she muttered. Then as she turned to leave, she whispered under her breath, 'some ghosts are made up from memory, others from guilt.'

Eliza wanted to ask her what that meant and why she said it, but her voice was nowhere to be heard or used. The door shut before she could say a thing.

That night Eliza could not sleep. The storm had been around Greywick for weeks and it was finally gone but now it was too quiet. She walked down the corridors barefoot in her lace nighty listening to the ticking of the clocks. The wallpaper seemed to move with the candlelight and sometimes she thought she heard whispering as faint as a page turning. In the hallway near the nursery, she noticed one brick looked different to the rest, it looked loose. She pressed her fingers against it, and it moved. Behind it was a thin, crumpled piece of paper… stained red from the brick's residue.

It was a drawing. A child's drawing of three people: a woman with a bun, a tall man beside her and a small circle with stick arms. Underneath in wonky handwriting were the words:

Maid Lissy dada

Eliza stared at it, her heart pounding. Who drew it? And how did they know?

She took it back to her room and placed it on her desk. She continued to stare at it for a long time. Then she reached for her journal and started writing again… letters to her mother. She wrote about everything:

Clara calling her Lissy, the drawing on the wall, how the house acts as if it is alive. She included Lord Harrow and how he looks at her when he called her his own, and how every inch and corner of Greywick is silent like dust on a wet surface.

However, she never sent them of course. She neatly folded each letter and hid it under the floorboard. Every night the pile grew bigger.

A few days later, Lord Harrow mentioned that he would be away on business for three days. The estate felt different the second he left, lighter, like a sigh of relief. Lady Imogene seemed to have become alive instantly. She ordered fresh flowers, polished the silver in the estate, and sent invitations to half of the country.

By the evening, Greywick was full and happy again. There was music, perfume, and more people. Laugher was filling every room and hallway, something the estate has not heard or felt in years. Clara, however, was nowhere to be seen. Earlier on Eliza did hear a click of a lock, quiet but intentional but she did not mention anything. Lady Imogene had her reasons though she never voiced them.

Janet helped Eliza dress for the occasion.

'Hold still,' she said pulling the corset strings so tight Eliza could barely breathe. 'You have the figure for it just not the patience.'

The soft silk gown was one of Clara's, it was beautiful and shimmered blue in colour. Eliza's hair was pinned back into a plaited bun, her lips painted blood red and her eyes outlined in faint grey ink. When she saw herself in the mirror, she barely recognised who was staring back. For a moment, she looked like she belonged here.

Downstairs, the drawing room was buzzing. Men in waistcoats loitered around the piano, woman fanned themselves as if they were speaking code to them. When Eliza entered, several heads turned and pierced through her body. Some then smiled politely and others scowled in disapproval. Lady Imogene introduced her to the guests as "a friend of the family." The words hurt more than she had expected.

She smiled and played the part of answering every single question, laughing when it felt right and putting on a brave smile the whole time. A few of the guests seemed genuinely kind… one woman complimented her posture, and another complimented her gown. But a handful looked her up and down as if they were trying to decide what she was. Not noble. Not a servant. She was something in between that made them uncomfortable.

The whole evening felt fake, every word that left her mouth felt rehearsed and every smile she received seemed to hide something. Everything she knew was a lie sewn together with silence and clear thread.

When the last guest left the estate it quietened abruptly, from so much noise to nothing in a split second. Eliza stayed in the drawing room to catch her thoughts for a second about everything that happened.

Her ribs ached from the corset, and her head was dizzy from the smell of wine and perfume. She had almost convinced herself she belonged there for a moment, but when the doors closed and all fell silent, she felt the walls closing back in on her angrily.

When she finally went upstairs her bedroom door was already open. Eliza crept in and found Clara sat on her bed, knees tucked to her chest with her hair flopping over her face. Her eyes were glassed over but she smiled straight when Eliza came in.

'Did you have fun?' She asked quietly.

Eliza did not answer, she sat next to her instead unpinning her hair and pulling the laces on the corset so she could breathe.

After a while Clara laid down and pulled the blanket around her.

'Do not leave me again.' She whispered.

Eliza stayed still for a long time staring up at the ceiling while Clara was fast asleep. She did not know if Clara meant do not leave her alone tonight or do not leave her ever. Maybe both. Either way, Eliza did not move.

Chapter Fifteen

Who was it?

June 1816

Eliza sat at her desk writing another letter she would never send. Her pen had barely touched the page when the sound appeared… wheels and hooves crunching over gravel. No one ever came to Greywick unannounced. She went to the window pushing the curtain aside. A dark carriage had stopped at the gates, the horses looked tired as if they had travelled a long way. The driver jumped down first shouting something to the gatekeeper, then the door opened.

A woman stepped out

For a long moment, Eliza thought she was going crazy and seeing things. The woman wore a faded cloak with dust clinging on tightly. She brushed her outfit and fixed her crooked bonnet. But even from the window Eliza knew. She knew the shape of her, the body language and everything else about her.

Her mother: Maggie, well Margaret.

Eliza's whole body felt ice cold and she could barely stand.

'This is not real. She is not there.' Eliza whispered to herself.

For a moment she considered running downstairs but something inside of her froze. Fear or disbelief… she did not know which. She heard voices coming from downstairs. It was a man calling for Lady Harrow, then a slam of a door followed by footsteps moving so quick it could be someone running, Then the sound of a stranger in the hallway.

'Goodness me… it is you.' Janet cried.

Eliza's breath disappeared. She moved impulsively without a thought of what she was doing, but instead of going downstairs she did the opposite. She ran away from the noise.

She ran so fast to the far wing where unused rooms stood thick with dust. The air was cooler there, full of cobwebs and the smell of old damp wood coated in years of abandonment. She pressed her back against a door and slid slowly to the floor. Eliza could still hear faint sounds of voices. Hers. Maggie's. It was all too much, too real. She had written her hundreds of letters in secret, and now she was here… at Greywick, she was too scared to say hello.

She pulled her knees to her chest pressing her forehead against them. For the first time since coming to Greywick, Eliza did not know what she wanted. To see her, or to disappear.

It was almost an hour before she moved.

The house had gone quiet, so Eliza stood up, brushed the dust off her dress, and made her way downstairs. Eliza entered the garden. The once green carefully mowed lawn had turned to a pale gold colour from the heat and lack of rain recently. The flowers all drooped and petals curled brown at the edges.

Maggie stood by the sundial, her back to house with one hand resting against the stone wall. When Maggie turned, her eyes were wet though she did not cry.

'Eliza!' She screamed softly, her voice shaking. 'Oh, my child. My little girl.'

Eliza froze. Every part of her wanted to run to Maggie and give her a long tight hug but another part held her captive unable to move.

'Why are you here, mother?' Eliza questioned

Maggie stepped closer. 'Isaac. He sent a letter from the estate to see you.'

Eliza did not hide her furrowed brows. 'Isaac…?'

'He is a friend of mine.' Maggie said quickly.

The sun was beating down on the estate and sweat was dripping down Eliza's neck.

'You shouldn't've come.' She whispered.

'I had to!' Maggie replied. 'When I heard about everything that has been going on. Good God Eliza! I was scared I would lose you to this place.'

'You did lose me' Eliza hastily responded. 'When you lied to me.'

Maggie flinched, 'I didn't lie to you.'

'You didn't tell me,' Eliza's tone got angrier and firmer. 'You could have said who he was. You could have said what this place really was before I left.'

Maggie shook her head, eyes welling up. "I wanted to protect you, my girl.'

'From what?'

'From him. From what it means to be a Harrow.' Maggie reluctantly whispered.

The family name came out like poison. Maggie took another step forward, her cloak dragging through the dry grass.

'You were never meant to come back here. I told you before you left, I warned you.'

Eliza's voice trembled in anger or worry; she was not sure how to feel. 'You should have told me the truth. ALL of it!'

Maggie looked down fidgeting with her hands. 'The truth would have kept you awake at night. It would have made you wonder who you were and what part of him lived inside your blood. I could not do that to you; I could not let you see the darkness I saw.'

Silence filled the estate's grounds.

When Maggie finally spoke again, her voice was powerless; nothing but a whisper.

'If he thinks he owns you again, he will take you. Just like he took everything else.'

Eliza looked up abruptly. 'What do you mean?'

Maggie's eyes locked on the estate. 'You think he does not remember what he has done? He does not see you as a person, Eliza. He sees what was stolen from him… like an object. And men like him do not stop until they get it back.'

'You think he'll hurt me?' Eliza stuttered with flushed cheeks and wide eyes.

'I think he already is. There's barely anything of you!' Maggie answered.

Eliza swallowed hard, like a golf ball had to fit down her throat. 'You should leave.'

Maggie shook her head repeatedly. 'Not without you!'

'I can't,' Eliza said. 'Not yet. There is more here. I can feel it.'

'There's nothing here worth finding.' Maggie said bitterly through her clenched teeth.

Eliza thought of the sketch hidden in her room: the drawing of the maid, the man, and the baby. Maid, Lissy, Dada. She thought of Clara asleep beside her that night whispering 'do not leave me again.'

'Maybe that's why I have to stay,' Eliza said softly. 'Because no one ever finishes the story, they just hide it.'

Maggie reached for her hand. 'Please. You do not understand what you are dealing with.' She begged.

Eliza hesitated, then took her hand. The touch felt weird. Warm but distant. For the first time, Maggie smiled at her.

'When you were born,' she whispered, 'I thought the world had finally given me something good. You were so small, so perfect. He looked at you and said you were mine to keep. But I heard the way he said it. It was as if he was giving me something broken.'

Tears rolled down her cheeks like rain running down a window. 'So, I ran, I left with nothing but you.'

Eliza felt her body ache in sorrow. 'You should've told me, mother.'

'I know, Darling." Maggie could barely speak at this point. 'But I thought if you did not know who you were, maybe you could be anyone you wanted to be. And free.'

They stood there for a long time, hands interlinked, the estate standing behind them like it was listening in. The golden sun sunk leaving soft autumn colours spilling over the horizon. A reminder of the seasons to come. When Maggie finally let go, Eliza felt the loss immediately.

'I'll stay nearby,' Maggie stated. 'Just for a few days, if you change your mind…'

Eliza nodded. 'I'll find you.'

Maggie brushed her fingers across Eliza's face. "My brave girl!' she murmured.

She turned and walked away, her cloak training through the hay-like grass. Eliza stood there long after the carriage had gone, staring at the gates. Her mind was racing, wondering if she chose the right path or if she has gone completely insane. When Eliza turned to look at the house, she thought she saw a figure standing in one of the windows. Just for a moment. Watching her.

Then it was gone and all fell silent.

Chapter Sixteen

The Darkness We Inherit

The storm never came that night, though the air felt like one was hiding somewhere close. The next morning was heavy and still, the kind of quiet that makes even the walls seem to listen.

Eliza woke to the faint sound of voices in the hall. Lady Imogene's voice trembling, a man's lower and sharp. She sat up, her pulse quickening. When she stepped out, the conversation stopped. Footsteps drifted away, and then the house fell into its usual hush.

At breakfast, no one spoke at all. Clara picked at her porridge. Lady Imogene looked pale, as if she had aged overnight. Lord Harrow had not yet returned from town, or so Eliza thought, until she saw him at the far end of the table, already seated, a folded stack of papers beside his plate.

He did not look up when she entered.

'Eliza,' he said, his tone firm but calm. 'Join us.'

She did, though her stomach had already knotted. He only glanced at her once, then returned to his meal, cutting each piece of meat with careful precision. When the meal ended, he stood, gathered the papers, and said, 'Study, now.'

The study was dim, curtains half drawn. Dust floated in the shafts of light. When the door shut behind them, Eliza realised Lady Imogene had not followed. It was only her and Lord Harrow.

'Your mother came here while I was away.' Lord Harrow said while placing papers on the table smoothing them out with his hand.

Eliza's chest pounded. 'I know. She came to visit me.'

His eyes looked up immediately. 'You saw her?' His eyes widening in surprise.

'She found me,' she replied. 'In the garden.'

He nodded slow. 'Then you know the truth. I have nothing left to hide.'

'You have both hidden enough.' Eliza crossed her arms and glowered at him across the desk.

He ignored Eliza's remark and pushed the papers towards her. 'This is an agreement,' he spoke loudly. 'It names you as my heir. Greywick will belong to you when I am gone. The estate, the lands, the title.'

She stared at the page. 'Why now?'

'Because' he said, lowering his voice, 'you are my blood, and I will not see my name die out in scandal. You deserve what is yours.'

Eliza almost laughed but merely smirked at him. 'You want me to be yours now, but not when I was born?' His face changed…guilt or anger, she could not tell.

'I was wrong then,' he whispered. 'But I can make it right again.'

Her hands shook as she read the words written in dark smudged ink. Then she saw the note near the bottom, underlined in his own handwriting: In exchange for inheritance, Miss Eliza Harrow relinquishes all claim to the woman known as Margaret Fell.

Her stomach turned as fast as earth orbiting. 'You mean I have to disown my mother?!'

He said nothing.

'Never!' she shouted.

'Eliza…'

'No!' Her voice broke through his. 'You do not get to fix what you destroyed. You do not get to buy forgiveness.'

The colour drained from his face. 'You don't understand what this means.'

'I understand perfectly,' she said, tearing the papers straight down the middle. The sound of the rip echoed like thunder in the quiet room.

Lord Harrow's chair scraped back violently. He slammed his fist against the desk. The glass ink bottle shattered, splattering black across the floorboards. 'You stupid girl!'

Clara appeared in the doorway, eyes wide.

Lord Harrow turned toward her, but before he could speak, she picked up the nearest object (a glass tumbler) and threw it. It hit the wall behind him and shattered. She grabbed the silver tray next, the candlestick, anything she could reach, hurling each with shaking hands.

'Stop it!' Lady Imogene's voice echoed from the hall, but Clara was already crying, half-screaming. 'You do not deserve her! You do not deserve anyone!'

When Lord Harrow tried to approach, she launched herself at him, pummelling his chest repeatedly with her tiny fists. The papers scattered, the chair toppled, and then she ran. The door slammed. Silence followed, broken only by the sound of glass crunching under his boots.

Eliza stood still, breathing hard. Her father's hand was bleeding where it had met the glass.

'She is her mother's child,' he muttered. 'So much fire where there should have been obedience.'

'As am I. She didn't love you,' Eliza said quietly. 'And neither do I.'

His gaze snapped to her.

'You don't get to own people,' she said, her voice steady now. 'Especially the ones you don't love.'

He stared at her for a long moment, something unreadable in his eyes…hatred, maybe. Or shame. Then he turned away.

Eliza left the study. Her hands would not stop shaking. When she reached her room, the corridor felt colder than usual.

That night, the house did not sleep. A faint smell crept through the halls, smoke. Not of the open kitchen hearth, but something else. Something secret. She followed it. Past the main staircase, down the long corridor leading to the east wing. The air grew hazy, warm. Someone had lit a fire there again. Through a crack in the door, she saw the flicker of orange light swallowing the walls. It was not raging, not yet just burning quietly, like someone trying to get rid of something piece by piece.

When she pushed the door open further, the smell thickened. The room was nearly empty except for old furniture and a cradle half hidden under a linen sheet. The flames were crawling up a pile of papers and cloth.

Eliza stepped forward, the heat licking her skin. She saw a fragment of writing catch fire, a name, her name, then disappear into ash.

She backed away, trembling. She remembered what Maggie had said.

If he thinks he owns you again, he will take you like he took everything else.

And now, he was trying to burn what little proof remained.

The fire crackled softly, almost gently.

Chapter Seventeen

Little Lark

Rain had fallen overnight, soft, and steady, and the scent of damp ash lingered in the corridors of Greywick. Eliza rose before the bells, her reflection pale and unsure in the mirror, her eyes carrying something harder now, something she had earned. She dressed without a thought, lacing her own corset, her hands steady even though her heart was not. When she left her room, the hallway was dim, the candles half-burnt from the night before. As she turned the corner toward the east corridor, she noticed Lady Imogene standing in the doorway of her chamber, her back to the light. Her hair was loose, and in her hands, she held a folded letter, the edges torn, the wax broken.

'He never loved either of us,' Imogene said, her voice as fragile as porcelain. She did not look up. The words were meant for no one and everyone.

Eliza stepped closer, her shoes barely sounding on the floorboards. 'What is that?'

Imogene held out the letter. Her fingers trembled slightly. 'His will.'

Eliza froze, staring at the paper as if it might catch flame just by being seen. 'His will?'

Imogene nodded once. 'He left it in the study drawer. I read it.' A bitter laugh escaped her. 'When he dies, he intends to leave everything. The estate. The title. The name. But there is a condition. If you refuse, you will never be free of him. If you accept, you will live under his name forever.'

Eliza took the letter. The parchment was thick, almost waxy with age. His handwriting looped across the page in dark, decisive strokes. She read enough to understand what it meant. To be his in name. To carry his blood publicly, proudly, as though the past had been something noble. Clara's voice came softly from the doorway, her hair undone, her small hands clutched around the banister. 'Would you really make him die?' she asked.

Eliza turned sharply, startled. 'Clara, you shouldn't…'

Clara stepped forward. 'Would you?'

Eliza lowered the letter, her throat tight. 'I'd let the past die,' she said slowly. 'Not a person.'

The answer did not seem to soothe the girl. Clara's eyes flicked from her half-sister to the letter, then to the floor.

'He is already dead inside,' she whispered. And then she was gone, down the stairs, her nightgown brushing the steps like a ghost descending. Lady Imogene following in her wake. The pair of them like wraiths in the daylight.

Eliza stood for a long moment in the silence that followed. She could hear the faint groan of the house, the kind that came with storms, and she thought about Maggie, about the years stolen between them. About all the things said and unsaid. She returned to her room where she folded the will carefully and placed it on the table beside the bed.

That evening, the library smelled of dust and candle oil. Shadows pooled beneath the shelves like spilled ink. Eliza walked along the rows, brushing her fingers over the spines of books she had once been too afraid to touch. Austen, Addison, Milton, Locke. Their names stared back at her like old judges.

A sound came from the doorway. It was a quiet knock, followed by the low creak of hinges. Isaac stood there, cap in hand, his boots wet from the yard. He looked uneasy, as though he had rehearsed something a dozen times and still was not sure he should say it.

'Miss Fell,' he said softly.

Eliza turned. 'Isaac. What is it?'

He closed the door behind him and stepped closer. The rain had left his coat dark and heavy. 'There's something ya need a know,' he said.

Her heart skipped a beat. 'Go on.'

'You were just a baby,' he began, his voice deep with the weight of the memory, 'when your mother left Greywick in the December of 1800. Lord Harrow had her sent away with ya. Paid her to leave.'

Eliza stared at him. The world seemed to have had a new door unopened. 'He paid her?'

'Aye.' Isaac nodded slowly. 'Said it was for her good. Said the house did not need trouble.' He hesitated, then reached into his pocket. It was a small wooden carving of a bird, its wings half open, its edges smoothed by time. 'This was yours,' he said. 'It was left behind. Found it in the old nursery years back. Lady

Imogene said it was to be burnt, but I could not bring myself to do it.'

Eliza took the carving carefully. It was a lark, her mother's favourite bird. The beak was slightly chipped, the wood darkened by age, but unmistakably hers. She ran her thumb along its wing. 'I was removed,' she whispered. 'To be safe.'

Isaac nodded once. 'Seems that way.'

The clock ticked steadily in the background. In that moment, the house did not feel like stone and bricks, but it felt like a living thing. Breathing, remembering, watching.

Eliza looked up, her eyes glistening and with a feeling of something she could not quite put her finger on. 'Thank you, Isaac.'

He tipped his cap. 'Be careful, Miss. Some ghosts ain't meant to rest.' Then he left her there, the rain trickling against the windowpanes, the air thick with old dust.

Eliza stood alone in the half-lit room holding the carved lark in between her palms. For the first time, the silence did not scare her. It felt almost like truth, it was fragile, imperfect, and finally her own.

Chapter Eighteen

Hot is Cold

The summer had come heavy and close this year, the kind that made the walls of Greywick seem to breathe. Curtains stuck to the windows, the air clung to skin, and every step down the corridor stirred a faint, baked scent of dust and polish. Outside, the fields were yellowing, the grass grown coarse and brittle under the sun. Even the crows had gone quiet.

Eliza woke most mornings with her hair damp against her neck and her sheets tangled. The house, despite its size, felt smaller in the heat. The air did not move; it just lingered like a held breath. Clara had taken to lying on the cool stone floor of the drawing room, her sketchbook open, her pencil moving lazily over the paper. Lady Harrow spent her afternoons fanning herself by the window and scolding the servants for not drawing the blinds quickly enough.

But there was one absence that unsettled Eliza more than the weather: Isaac.

For days she had not seen him crossing the lawns or trimming the hedges. No sound of his boots on the gravel, no soft whistle from the orchard. It was unusual. He was a man who rose with the dawn and worked until the light was gone. By the fifth day, something in her needed to check it out.

She left the main house and crossed the yard, the heat shimmering off everything. The small servants' cottage stood half-sunk into the earth in an almost impenetrable stand of trees close to the stables which kept it hidden from view of the main house, with a small brook weaving between the trees. Its thatched roof was patchy, its walls were cracked and grey. When she opened the door, a wave of cold hit her so sharply it made her gasp for air.

It should not have been cold. Not in this heat.

The air inside was wrong, stale and chilly as if it had forgotten the season. The single window was sealed with grime, the hearth empty, the floor bare. Isaac lay on the narrow bed underneath a threadbare blanket shivering violently. His skin had turned the colour of parchment, his lips tinged blue and purple.

'Isaac?' Eliza rushed to his side, pressing a hand to his forehead. He burned with fever.

He stirred, his breath shallow. 'Didn't… mean to worry you, Miss,' he rasped. 'Just the cold, that's all.'

'The cold?' she repeated, looking around the room. It felt like a cellar, all warmth drained away. She hurried back to the house to find Janet. They returned with broth, blankets, and candles that barely stayed lit in the strange chill.

They sat him up, spooned the broth slowly past his lips. Janet rubbed his hands between hers, muttering prayers under her breath. 'He's a good man,' she said. 'Always was. Do not deserve this house's curse.'

Eliza frowned. 'Curse?'

Janet hesitated. 'It takes the gentle ones first.'

The next day Lady Imogene appeared at the doorway, her gown untouched by dust, her face pale but composed. She stood for only a moment, looking at Isaac with something like discomfort. 'That is where servants shall live, no matter what,' she said coldly. 'They shall not live with us. They are too… common.'

Eliza stared at her. 'He's dying.'

'Then pray he doesn't,' Imogene replied offhandedly before turning away and gliding back to the house.

When Eliza later approached and told Lord Harrow that Isaac was really ill, he barely looked up from his papers. 'You are neglecting your teaching duties,' he said sharply. 'The child's lessons matter more than a servant's fever. Servants come and go.'

She wanted to scream at him. Instead, she left the room and did not return until nightfall.

For two more days, Isaac drifted between sleep and delirium. Clara sat by his bed each afternoon, sketchbook balanced on her knees, drawing the twisted apple tree visible through the window. She did not say much, only glanced up every so often and whispered, 'It is still growing, see? It has not given up.' Isaac would nod faintly, a ghost of a smile crossing his cracked lips.

On the fourth night, the fever broke. The cold began to lift. Janet lit the hearth and the warmth seemed to spread at last, creeping back into the room like forgiveness. Eliza stayed beside him until dawn. When Isaac opened his eyes fully again, they were clearer, though sunken. He looked at her and smiled weakly.

'You frightened me,' Eliza said, her voice shaking.

He coughed a laugh. 'Did not mean to. Just needed a rest, maybe.'

She leaned forward. 'You were the first person who ever told me the real truth about this place.'

He nodded slowly, voice barely above a whisper. 'That truths not finished yet.' Before closing his eyes and going back into a restful sleep. When he awoke a couple of hours later, Eliza found out the reason the cottage was so cold. Originally, Lord Harrow was thinking about making an icehouse which was fashionable for keeping things cold when entertaining. That particular spot remained so cold all year round with the shade of the trees and a water source. They got as far as digging a trench but realised that the brook wouldn't provide adequate water, as it could run very low at times, so they sourced an alternative which was also closer to the kitchens and not so far from the main house and just slapped up the cottage instead which was poorly maintained.

The next afternoon, as the heat settled over the estate again, a carriage arrived. The sound of hooves breaking the dry earth made everyone turn. The horses were dark, their harnesses gleaming, and the man who stepped down was dressed entirely in black. He carried a leather satchel and an envelope sealed with red wax.

He asked for Miss Fell.

Eliza met him in the front hall, her hands still dusty from the garden. The man removed his hat, his face unreadable.

'I've come from the Town Council in Godalming,' he said. 'Concerning your employment here.'

He handed her the sealed letter.

Her pulse quickened. 'My employment?'

He told her the Town Council in Godalming had learned of her through the estate's own records. Each year, the estate was expected to send word of those living and working on its grounds, and her name had appeared. One of Isaac's letters, carried into town by post, had also mentioned her directly. The council had no memory of her arrival, nor record of her origin, and no notice that she had entered service. It was their duty, he said, to account for those employed within their bounds. He had been sent to deliver their letter and to see who she was.

He nodded once. 'They've raised… questions, Miss. Questions about your name. And your right to be here.'

Eliza stared at the letter, the wax gleaming like blood in the light. Behind her, she could feel the house holding its breath again, the same stillness as before a storm.

The lark carving in her pocket felt suddenly heavy, as if reminding her that the truth always comes, no matter how deep it is buried.

Chapter Nineteen

The Air Before a Storm

The heat settled over Greywick like a burning quilt that no one could lift. By July, the days stretched unbearably long, the sort of hours that melted into one another until morning and afternoon felt the same. The sun baked the lawns to a brittle yellow, and the gravel paths shimmered as if swallowing light. Even the birds seemed exhausted. They perched with open beaks and slow, anxious blinking, as though the world had grown too hot to sing in.

Inside, the house felt even more heavy. It was thick with warmth, thick with silence, thick with something unspoken.

Eliza spent most mornings tutoring Clara, though Clara's attention wandered probably because of how hot it was. She fidgeted with her quill. She drew shapes on the paper instead of letters. She stared at the window instead of her books. Some days she would whisper, 'When will summer end? I cannot breathe here.' Other days she was quiet and jumpy, flinching whenever footsteps were heard in the hall.

Eliza tried to keep lessons gentle. But Clara kept slipping further away, as if someone were pulling strings behind her back and she was too tired to resist.

When their sessions were over, Eliza retreated to the gardens, where the apple trees drooped in the heat, or to her room where she could close the door and pretend, just for a moment, that Greywick was not watching her. She used the warmth as her excuse. Nobody questioned it. The whole house slept like a creature that did not want to wake.

Lord Harrow, however, seemed alert.

He appeared more often in the corridors, hands clasped neatly behind his back, his expression softened to a polite interest that made her skin prickle. He asked how the lessons went. He asked how her health was. He asked whether she slept well, ate enough, felt "comfortable" here.

His manners were smooth, but beneath them she sensed something gathering…something patient and calculating.

Lady Imogene, meanwhile, behaved impeccably whenever others could see her. She moved through the house with grace, greeting guests, nodding to servants, smiling when required.

But behind closed doors Eliza heard the arguments, the frustrated hissing that slipped out like steam from boiling water.

Clara was kept close. Too close. Locked in her room on some days, escorted by Imogene on others. She never complained aloud; she only grew quieter.

And the servants… changed.

They did their work, but they avoided Eliza's eyes. Even Janet, loyal Janet, moved through the corridors like she was avoiding her. Once Eliza tried to speak to her (just a simple good morning), but Janet turned away too quickly, muttering something about linens and duty. Her shoulders trembled ever so slightly.

That was the day Eliza found the rose.

It appeared on her windowsill at dawn: a single red bloom, its petals full, its stem thorny. It sat there like a warning…beautiful, deliberate, dangerous.

Isaac had used roses before apparently. Years ago, when the estate's tensions were sharp and unpredictable, he had left one to signal caution to some of the staff. Thorn for danger. Colour for urgency. A rose meant: be careful what you touch. Even soft things cut.

Eliza held the flower in her hand and felt the meaning charge through it.

Someone was watching. Someone was deciding something. And Isaac wanted her to know.

Later that day, while the house napped in the heat, she felt eyes on her again. Not imagined ones. Real ones. They flickered from the upper windows when she crossed the garden. They appeared in the long corridor mirror, just a shadow behind her shoulder, gone when she turned. They lingered outside the schoolroom during lessons. Whoever it was did not bother hiding well.

By evening she discovered her private notes, diary pages, small letters she drafted but never sent… moved from where she had put them. They were not missing, only moved. She stood by the desk, hands trembling, trying to understand how someone could enter so quietly.

She could not accuse anyone. She could not prove anything. But the intrusion settled under her skin like a bruise.

The estate itself grew tense. Every creak felt louder. Every whisper travelled further.

At supper, Lord Harrow approached her with an easy smile that never once touched his eyes.

'Miss Fell,' he said, 'join me tomorrow evening. A private dinner to discuss your future here.'

His tone was light, but his gaze was not.

Eliza kept her voice steady. 'I must prepare Clara's lessons.'

'Lessons,' he repeated, amused. 'On a summer evening?'

'She's falling behind,' Eliza said firmly.

He watched her for a long moment, and she felt again that sense of being studied like a puzzle he believed he could solve.

Then he inclined his head. 'Very well. Another time.'

The refusal did not feel victorious. It felt like lighting a match in the rain.

That night, when the house finally lay quiet, Eliza stepped out onto the balcony. The sky was turning the colour of honey as dusk settled. The garden, yellowed and tired, stretched beneath her like a living map of every secret the estate had tried to bury.

The air was still, so still it seemed to hush even her own breath. She held the rose in her hand, the stem wrapped carefully so the thorns would not pierce her skin. Somewhere inside the house a door creaked. Somewhere down the hall, a floorboard sounded.

Something was coming. She felt it in the heat, in the walls, in the silence.

For the first time since arriving at Greywick, fear grew inside her.

Chapter Twenty

Dolls in a Playhouse

No one spoke it aloud, but the walls felt thin, stretched, trembling. Sound travelled differently, sharper, quicker, as if the house itself were eager to tell secrets.

Lord Harrow's presence was strange recently.

He had always been a shadow lingering at the edge of rooms, but now he moved with the confidence of a man who believed he owned every breath beneath his roof. Eliza noticed him everywhere, in doorways, on stairwells, at the far end of the gardens where she had thought to herself that she was alone. His comments came coated in politeness, but the rot underneath was unmistakable.

'You look flushed, Miss Eliza,' he remarked one afternoon, gaze staying far too long. 'The summer is unkind to delicate things.'

She kept her chin lifted. 'Some things only wilt when handled improperly.'

His smile sharpened. A cat's smile. A collector's smile.

Clara watched these interactions like a hawk, her concerns grew though she pretended otherwise. Her loyalties tangled inside her like thread pulled too tightly; one moment she hovered near Eliza with her teaching her, the next she snapped back beneath her mother's expectations. But she was not careful about hiding her feelings anymore, her rebellion showed in flashes. Clara flinched when her father entered a room. She clenched her jaw when he addressed Eliza.

Eliza did not blame her. Greywick was a place built on contradictions, devotion that bled and loyalty that bruised.

In the servant's wing, a separate story unfolded. Janet entered Lord Harrow's study one morning with linens, expecting nothing more sinister than a cluttered desk. Instead, she froze. On the corner of that immaculate mahogany surface lay something small enough to be overlooked but impossible to forget: a scrap of fabric, torn and stiff with dried blood. Not new. Old enough that the brown had faded at the edges. A button still clung to one corner.

Too small to belong to any man. Not fitting any clothing in the house.

Janet went colourless. Her hands trembled even as she quietly slipped the scrap into her apron. She said nothing. That was the rule. The servant's house, separate from the main estate, had secrets by the dozen, but that night she hid the fabric in a tin beneath her bed, as if burying it would stop its truth from becoming known.

When Eliza next saw her, Janet would not look at her.

Isaac found her by the horse paddock late one afternoon listlessly watching the foals following their overheated mothers. Thunder murmured distantly, the first sign of a storm after weeks of blistering heat. He brushed past her as if by accident, eyes forward, voice low.

'The estate doesn't stay quiet forever.'

A warning disguised as pretend conversation. His version of leaving a rose without leaving a rose.

Eliza's breath caught. 'Isaac…'

He shook his head. 'Not here.'

Nothing more.

But the sky tightened overhead like a fist closing.

It happened in the hallway outside the music room.

Lord Harrow reached forward and touched a strand of Eliza's hair, nothing more than the lightest brush, but enough. Enough to freeze Eliza. Enough to make her skin crawl and her heart surge into her throat. Enough to make the air taste like iron.

He said softly, 'It suits you down.'

Eliza stepped back, spine rigid. But the true eruption came from behind them.

Lady Imogene made a sound that did not belong to a polite aristocratic society. Something raw and vicious. She grabbed Clara by the arm with such force that she yelped. The slap cracked across the hallway, echoing off marble and wood. Clara stood still with tears flooding her eyes instantly.

'You ungrateful girl,' Lady Imogene hissed, though the words were not really for Clara at all.

Then she disappeared. Vanished into her chambers, the door slamming so hard a framed painting rattled. She would not appear for three days. Food trays left untouched. Curtains drawn. Servants whispering that she might have smashed a mirror, or two, or all of them.

Eliza knew better.

Grief did strange things to women who had been taught never to scream.

By the time, the storm broke, Greywick was suffocating.

Rain crashed down in sheets thick enough to distort the world into blurred silhouettes. Thunder bloomed over the estate, loud, theatrical, the earth itself cracking open. Trees bent low under the weight of wind. Flowers in the garden trembled, petals torn clean off by the violence of it.

Eliza stood at her bedroom window and watched the downpour swallow the grounds. Her candle flickered wildly in the draft. The storm felt like the release of something the entire estate had been holding for months. Maybe the start of releasing a secret.

She pressed a hand to the glass. Somewhere deep inside her, a truth surfaced: 'They were never daughters,' she whispered, repeating something she had once overheard a governess say about wealthy children. 'Just dolls in someone else's playhouse.'

Clara. Herself. Lady Imogene. Even the servants.

All of them arranged and repositioned on impulse, a whim.

Lord Harrow grew stern after the storm, as if the thunder had cleansed the last shreds of politeness from him. His comments sharpened into something unmistakable; the power became visible.

One evening he murmured, 'You mistake me, Miss Eliza. What I feel for you is… considerable.'

She replied, calm but icy, 'He called it love. She called it survival.'

He laughed softly. The sound of a man who did not like being told a truth he could not control.

Clara found Eliza late that night outside the library. The girl's face was blotchy, eyes swollen, her voice choked.

'Miss Eliza… I think he is going to…' She cut herself off, shaking her head violently. 'I am scared.'

Eliza knelt, taking Clara's trembling hands and looked into her eyes.

'You are not alone.'

'But he watches you,' Clara whispered. 'And Mama is not… she is not… she will not help.'

Clara's fear was not childish. It had the weight of witnessing too much.

Eliza walked out to the balcony, still slick with rain. The lamps below cast the gardens in thin, ghostly gold light. A mist rises from the drenched earth like breath from a sleeping beast.

Something is coming.

She feels it in the air, in the walls, in the tremor running through her own ribs. The fear settles in her like an unwelcome guest staying too long.

She stands there until the last rumble of thunder fades. Alone. Watched. And brutally aware that the storm outside was only a show in comparison to the one brewing inside.

Chapter Twenty-One

The Last Meal

Candlelight danced across polished silver and porcelain, casting wavering shadows on the damask walls. Crystal glasses clinked, roast meat steamed on platters, and yet beneath all of this something unspoken drifted through the room as delicate as lace and as tense as a wire.

The estate felt different that evening, as though Greywick itself were holding its breath waiting for something to happen.

Hours earlier, Eliza had slipped into Lord Harrow's study…not boldly, not foolishly, but with the dread of someone who already knew what she would find.

The room smelled of pipe smoke, polish, and something metallic she could not quite place her finger on. She opened drawers methodically, her fingers trembling only when she found an envelope marked with her name that had never been delivered. Next came sketches, portraits of her as a child she did not remember posing for, rough charcoal drawings of an infant, detail impossibly precise: the birthmark behind her ear, the curl of pale hair. Letters addressed to "The Harrow Child."

A lock of baby hair tied with blue ribbon. Documents noting payments to "M. Fell."

Her stomach hollowed.

It was all real. Every suspicion, every whisper, every fragment of the truth Isaac and Janet had tried to give shape to.

Then the last drawer, the one she had to pry open carefully so the wood would not splinter. It held a small wooden rattle painted lavender, worn smooth along the handle. Hers, she knew it in her gut. He had kept everything. Not from sentiment, but from ownership. Possession disguised as 'memory.'

Clara found her standing in the middle of the study, white-faced. Her hands were shaking.

'What are you doing in here?' Clara hissed, though fear replaced anger quickly.

Eliza showed her nothing, only said, 'You don't want to know.'

Clara squared her small shoulders like someone trying to feel bigger than they were. 'I do. I am not a child.'

So, Eliza told her enough to make Clara's lips go bloodless.

Clara stormed to her father's side of the house, a rare sighting of anger brewing and igniting in her. Eliza followed far behind, not to intervene, but to witness.

'Why did you not tell me she is…why did you not tell me who she is?' Clara demanded.

Lord Harrow barely glanced up from sorting his papers.

'You are confused,' he replied flatly. 'You have always been so sensitive. We must fix that.'

'That is not an answer,' Clara snapped.

He sighed as though she were the inconvenience. 'Your tutor fills your head with fantasies. That girl was nothing. She is nothing. And you are tired and overheated, that is all.' Gaslighting wrapped in silk.

Clara's rage then folded into fear, and she backed out of the room. She did not run. But she did not look back.

Janet intercepted Eliza in the corridor afterwards. Her face was pale, her eyes too bright.

'You need to leave,' she whispered. 'Tonight. Before he decides the walls should close again.'

She tugged Eliza by the wrist toward the servant stairwell, baskets waiting, a cloak hidden under a pile of linens. She had planned it, carefully.

They made it as far as the second-floor landing.

Lord Harrow stepped into the corridor from the shadows as though he had always been there, watching. Janet froze. Eliza felt the cold ripple up her spine.

'Going somewhere?' he asked mildly, like a teacher catching a child skipping lessons.

Janet tried to steady her breath. 'She needs air, my lord.'

'You are dismissed,' he said. 'Permanently. Get out!'

There was no plea in Janet's eyes, only heartbreak and an apology she did not say but clearly thought. She bowed her head and walked away.

Lord Harrow held Eliza by the arm, not hard, not bruising, and marched her to the guest wing.

He locked the door behind her. 'You will stay,' he said. 'Until supper.'

Alone, Eliza leaned her forehead against the cool door. She breathed slow, steady breaths. She did not feel like a child anymore from everything she now knows. She knew too much for a child. But she was also not helpless.

When Lady Imogene knocked later, she entered without waiting.

'Formal supper tonight,' she announced. Her face was pale, powdered too heavily, eyes rimmed red. 'You and Clara will attend. One final display of dignity.' The last word cut like a thread snapping.

Eliza did not argue. She simply nodded. She understood perfectly, this was not a dinner. This was a theatre.

She chose pale blue. A soft, icy colour that shimmered when the candlelight shone on it. Her hair pinned in soft waves around her shoulders. She looked, for one strange moment, like the portrait of the child she had once been.

Clara appeared dressed in black. No ribbons. No lace. Black like protest. Black like mourning. Her eyes flicked to Eliza's, full of determination and dread.

The dining hall was vast, and their steps echoed across the polished floor.

Lady Imogene sat rigid at the head of the table, her hands crushed together in her lap. The glass of wine trembled as she poured.

Lord Harrow arrived last.

Silent. Slow. Eyes fixed on Eliza as he walked the length of the table.

Candlelight licked the edges of his silhouette.

He sat. Lifted his glass.

'To obedience,' he said. 'And those who know their place… and those who forget.'

They dined like a family, but the knife did not just carve meat.

Cutlery chimed softly against porcelain. The grandfather clock ticked in metronome.

Lady Imogene tried to force small talk; her voice shook worryingly.

Clara stared at her plate.

Eliza kept her back straight, her chin level, her breath even.

Then came the remark.

'I brought you here to assist with your younger sisters education,' Lord Harrow provoked, carving slowly, deliberately. "After I had such glowing reviews from the parish council about how diligent you were as a person in terms of your manners and decorum, then this is how you repay me?'

Clara slammed her hands on the table. 'She is not your prisoner!'

Silence. The sort that swallows sound whole.

Lord Harrow stood. Slow. Controlled.

He walked behind Eliza's chair.

She did not move.

Flick of his wrist, swift like he had practiced for this moment, and the carving knife was in his hand.

Then it was at her throat.

The knife kissed her skin. A single drop of blood slid down her neck.

Lady Imogene choked on her drink, clutching her napkin to her mouth.

She did nothing. She always did nothing.

Clara shrieked, grabbed the nearest object, a wine bottle, and threw it at her father.

It shattered against the wall in a shower of dark red, staining the damask like blood.

'Leave her alone!' Clara screamed. 'Touch her again and I will… I will…' She did not finish the threat. She did not need to.

Lord Harrow lowered the knife, breathing heavily, but his eyes burned with a want to do more to Eliza. Everyone could see it.

Eliza lifted her napkin, dabbed the blood, and stood without asking to be excused.

Lady Imogene sipped on her soup, crying in a strange silent way.

Clara followed Eliza to the bedrooms, shaking. Neither spoke.

Later, when the house was dark and sleeping, Clara crept into Eliza's washroom and found the collar of the pale blue dress soaking in the basin.

A thin pink swirl seeped through the water.

She gathered it in her little hands, shaking with fury and sadness.

Downstairs, Eliza fed the fabric into the fireplace. Clara sat beside her, legs tucked under her, watching the flames eat the cloth.

'We cannot stay here,' Clara whispered.

'No,' Eliza said. Her gaze was steady; the fire reflected in her eyes. 'Tomorrow.'

'Where will we find oil? Or gas? To…' Clara swallowed. 'To burn it all?'

Eliza touched the small carved lark Isaac had given her, tucked warm in her pocket.

'Isaac collects oil lamps,' she said softly. 'Enough to finish it all.'

The flames crackled.

Eliza and Clara both went separately to their rooms with the knowledge that tomorrow will be the big day.

Chapter Twenty-Two

Where the New Start Begins

Eliza woke before the birds.

No dream or nightmare startled her awake; it was the heaviness in the air, the sense of something final stirring. Her throat stung where last night's knife had kissed her skin, a small throb that felt more like a reminder than a wound. She sat up slowly, listening to the house breathe its old, tired breath. Greywick had always groaned in the mornings, but this felt different… like the walls knew their time was short.

She dressed plainly, no silk, no pale blue satin. Just a simple gown she had mended herself months earlier, the sort of thing she had worn long before she knew she belonged to the Harrow bloodline. She braided her hair tightly, fingers steady despite the tremble in her organs.

When she opened her door, Isaac was already in the corridor. He did not speak. He did not need to. He gave her one small nod; the kind people exchange before doing something irreversible.

Together, they moved through Greywick as if they had done it a thousand times. They had not. But the house had always been a maze of secrets, and Eliza had learned its corridors like she learned grief, quietly, deeply, with no one noticing.

In his hands, Isaac carried the lamp oil box. She carried nothing yet; her hands needed to be free.

They began with the east wing.

Isaac uncapped the lamps and tipped the oil in slow glistening trails across the floorboards. The liquid ran in long, dark ribbons, soaking into the wood like it had been thirsty for years. Eliza worked beside him, dousing the corners, the rugs, the skirting boards.

Each splash was a promise and victory.

The early light was pale at the windows but outside the birds were already starting to chatter, completely unaware of what was happening and what will happen.

When Isaac stepped into Lord Harrow's study, Eliza froze. Lord Harrow was slumped at his desk, head leaning awkwardly on his hand, snoring faintly.

A man who believed himself too powerful to fear anything, not even fire in his own walls. Isaac looked at her once. Then he stepped back, pulled the door shut and quietly slid the heavy key into the lock.

He turned it. Locked in.

He did not speak; she did not either. Their silence said enough.

On her way back down the hall, Lady Imogene drifted into sight like a ghost wandering out at night. She was humming faint lullabies, the type she probably once sang to Clara before the weight of her marriage broke her down into shards.

Her hair was loose. She held an empty glass.

Milk, Eliza realised. She was going to fetch milk.

Imogene glanced down at the wet floor and frowned.

'Why is everything so damp?' she whispered.

Isaac managed to come up with the gentlest lie Eliza had ever heard.

'Because Janet is gone, my lady, and you've no maid. Thought I'd mop the floors for ya. Be careful, don't want ya to slip.'

To Eliza's surprise, Imogene smiled. A small, tired, almost loving smile.

'Thank you, Isaac.'

She stepped around the wet patch like someone walking through morning dew, not murder.

Eliza swallowed something sharp in her chest.

Clara was waiting in her room, already dressed, her hair plaited to the side. She had two bags packed on the bed neatly, purposeful bundles wrapped in cloth.

'I could not take everything…' she whispered.

'You have enough,' Eliza said gently.

Clara nodded, sighing hard.

'I packed one for you too. Just in case we actually make it.'

Eliza brushed a hand through Clara's hair. 'We will.'

Downstairs, the house was beginning to stir. A low creak here and there. As if the estate sensed what was coming.

Eliza slipped into the drawing room. Imogene was thankfully upstairs again. The curtains hung tall and heavy, decades old, the edges dry as hay. Eliza lit a candle, shielding the flame with her palm, then tucked it deep into the lining where the fabric pooled. One spark nestled itself against the curtain's underbelly.

It took at once.

Not violently. Almost shyly

The smallest thread glowed orange, then began to curl into smoke.

Heat whispered upward.

She did not watch long. She left the room as quietly as she had entered and went straight for the storage room. Another spark. Another room.

Then the old nursery.

She hesitated at that door, not for sentiment, there was none left for Greywick, but for the terrible knowledge of what had happened in that room long before her memory had formed.

She stepped in anyway.

And burned it too.

By the time she returned to the hall, the smoke had begun creeping in faint, thin ribbons under the doors.

A breath of warning.

Lord Harrow's voice rose from behind the study door, muffled, irritated.

'What the devil is this? Open this door! Do you hear me? OPEN THIS…'

Smoke seeped into his words. His coughing began sharply, violently.

Eliza did not stop walking.

Upstairs, Lady Imogene paused on the landing. Smoke curled around her ankles like a cat brushing for attention.

'What is happening?' she whispered.

She reached for the pistol kept in the cabinet at the top of the stairs, the one Lord Harrow thought she never knew about.

Eliza's heart stopped.

Imogene staggered into the corridor through smoke thick enough to sting the eyes. When she spotted Eliza, she squinted, lifted the gun, and fired. The shot echoed through the house.

The bullet buried itself in the wall.

Too much smoke. Too much shaking.

'Eliza!' Clara's voice shrilled from somewhere near the cellar.

Eliza ran.

She found Clara crying beside the old cellar door, clutching both bags in her small hands. Isaac appeared behind them, wiping soot from his brow.

'This way!' he rasped.

They did not look back.

The heavy door Eliza once stood outside of to come in was now their final goodbye with a slam.

They sprinted as fast as they could down the gravel road, the same one Eliza had first walked on months ago, frightened, unsure, and unaware of the truth of her blood.

Today, her feet hardly touched the ground.

The roar behind them rose higher, louder. Flames clawed at the sky. The windows burst one by one like shattering bones. Greywick burned as bright as a sunrise, a final monstrous gasp.

By the time they reached the iron gates, they all turned. Not because they needed to but because they deserved to. They deserved to see what they had managed to pull off and survive.

A house that had once been a tomb now collapsed inward like it was bowing.

It glowed red, then collapsed in places, beams falling, walls folding.

Clara was the first to laugh.

A wild, breathless thing.

Eliza joined her.

Even Isaac chuckled.

Tired and relieved.

Isaac adjusted his cap and smiled crookedly. 'I have somewhere to be, girls. But it was nice meetin' ya Eliza… and nice growin' with you Clara.'

He tipped his head and then he ran, vanishing down the road as though the smoke was carrying him away.

Clara and Eliza stood side by side, soot-stained, blood-dried, whole in a way neither had been before.

Eliza took Clara's hand.

They walked until the forest swallowed them, branches overhead weaving a green canopy above. Birds startled. Leaves whispered. The forest floor welcomed them like an old friend.

When they reached the clearing, the morning light had begun to break.

They collapsed into the tall, uncut grass. It cushioned them softly, the earth warm beneath their backs.

Eliza lay in the tall, uncut grass beside Clara, the wilderness tangled softly beneath her, still damp from the night's dew. It clung to her skin and sleeves: grounding. Above them, the sky stretched wide and just beginning to blush with the first light of the day. Soft pinks, bruised purples painted over the treetops like a quiet apology for what happened in the early hours.

She breathed. Shallow at first, then deeper, as though her lungs were learning the feeling of freedom and peace for the very first time.

'We're free,' she whispered, barely more than the wind through the leaves. Trembling and real.

Clara did not answer, just turned her head, eyes wide and shining with something between awe and disbelief.

Eliza smiled at her, ash on her cheeks, blood dried at her collar, hair loosely tangled in ribbons. Then, with everything that had not been burned away, her voice sounded alive:

'WE'RE FREE!'

The scream carried across the fields, not echoing, but lingering.

Behind them, Greywick died its final death.

A long, low groan, then nothing but smoke spiralling into the new day sky.

Eliza closed her eyes; fingers still entwined with Clara's.

The night swallowed the building whole; a suffocating breath of smoke where love lay buried beneath the ash… forever haunted by the secrets no flame could consume.

The silence was finally broken.

Adrenaline ran high in both Eliza and Clara. They have never felt this feeling before and now they do, they feel unstoppable. They feel as if they could change the world, but they are only children at the end of the day. Maybe they will not be able to, the world is big that is for sure.

They stared at the sky in awe, relief, and disbelief. Everything was now over; it never will be forgotten but it never will be relived.

This is the day that will always be remembered as the start to their futures.

Free.

Thank you to those who supported and believed in me every step of the way. And thank you to myself for finishing it even after all the doubt thinking I was not good enough, for trusting the process of writing and for not abandoning it when it would have been easier to stop.

www.ingramcontent.com/pod-product-compliance
Lightning Source LLC
LaVergne TN
LVHW091003080826
845145LV00003B/1108

9781067626709